It has to be a dream. Of course it's a dream.

Greg ran through room after room, the wooden floors creaking under his feet. He could hear the soldiers pounding along in pursuit.

A window appeared ahead, open wide. He stumbled as he ran the last few paces and peered outside, his lungs heaving, assessing the distance to the ground.

Then Greg looked up, toward Paris. His throat caught.

The city was gone.

The jammed streets, the tour boats, the cacophony of taxi horns and ambulance sirens . . . All of it had been replaced, except for Notre Dame, which now towered over everything else. The Seine was dark and untamed. Few of the buildings stood over two stories. The stagnant air was so quiet that Greg could hear the sound of horses' hooves and conversations on the other side of the river.

It wasn't a dream. It couldn't be. It felt too real.

He'd gone back in time.

Also by Stuart Gibbs

The Last Musketeer: Traitor's Chase
The Last Musketeer: Double Cross

THE LAST MUSKETEER

STUART GIBBS

HARPER

An Imprint of HarperCollinsPublishers

To my parents, who always encouraged me to dream

The Last Musketeer
Copyright © 2011 by HarperCollins Publishers
All rights reserved. Printed in the United States of America.
No part of this book may be used or reproduced in any manner
whatsoever without written permission except in the case of
brief quotations embodied in critical articles and reviews. For
information address HarperCollins Children's Books, a division
of HarperCollins Publishers, 195 Broadway,
New York, NY 10007.
www.harpercollinschildrens.com

Library of Congress Cataloging-in-Publication Data is available.
ISBN 978-0-06-285215-1

Typography by Erin Fitzsimmons
18 19 20 BRR 10 9 8 7 6 5 4 3 2 1
❖
Revised paperback edition, 2018

ACKNOWLEDGMENTS

WHEN I FIRST STARTED WRITING THIS BOOK, I KNEW almost nothing about life in medieval Europe or any French history before Napoleon. Thankfully, I had two awesome women to assist me in my studies. First, my dear friend Courtney Spikes fortuitously happens to be a professor of French history at Mount St. Mary's College. Then, Emily Mullin was not only an incredible researcher, but she also knew how to fence—and ultimately helped me craft this story. Their help was invaluable.

I am also deeply indebted to Daniel Ehrenhaft, who spearheaded this project and was essential to its development. Many of the great ideas in these pages are Dan's. Without him, this book wouldn't exist at all.

And finally, I need to thank my wife, Suzanne, who, in addition to all her usual wonderfulness, arranged a fantastic Paris vacation for us a few years ago—and didn't mind when I insisted spending part of it clambering around inside the bell towers of Notre Dame and exploring the medieval fortress in the basement of the Louvre. I had no idea I'd be writing this book at the time or that those excursions would ever be useful, but as you'll see, they were.

PROLOGUE

CLINGING TO THE PRISON WALL, GREG RICH REALIZED how much he hated time travel.

It wasn't just that he was trapped in the past—he was also trapped in midair a few feet below a sword-wielding guard with orders to kill him and a hundred feet above a clump of jagged rocks that would turn him into something resembling dog food if he fell.

Time travel should have been *fun*, right? Sure, you would have to survive without the internet and cell phones and ice cream, but you'd also get to experience the world before everyone had paved and polluted it. You could see famous places and people that you'd only read about.

(Unfortunately, as Greg had learned, you'd get to *smell* them, too.)

He definitely hadn't expected to *hate* time travel, mostly because he hadn't considered that time travel was possible in the first place. Then again, he hadn't expected he'd have to rescue his parents while on the run from the French army either. . . .

But there was no point in driving himself crazy over what had happened. Right now, Greg needed to keep still until the guard above him left his post. The problem was that his arms ached from holding on to the jagged stone, and his fingers were going numb from the pain. Gritting his teeth, he glanced out at the river that surrounded the prison. He squinted, searching for the other boys, but he saw only choppy waves glistening in the moonlight. If his new friends weren't on their way as planned, he was heading straight into a death trap.

Funny: He'd been in France only for four days. It felt like years. Maybe that was because, technically, it *was* years. The day he'd gone back in time was three days ago *and* four hundred years in the future. That was another problem with time travel: It scrambled your brain into mush.

Was he changing history, or had he somehow always been a part of it? Was he screwing up the future by being here? What if saving his parents now set off a chain of events that would ultimately negate his own existence?

Greg shook his head, chasing the thoughts away. *Focus on the positives. Concentrate on the task at hand: Rescue parents, and don't get killed.* Once he'd done that, he could consider the paradoxes of the time-space continuum—

There was a voice on the parapet above.

It didn't belong to the guard. In the near-silent night, sound carried easily; it was incredible how quiet the world in 1615 was after dark. Greg instantly recognized the deep, gravelly tone. A shiver shot down his spine. The madman was already here. The deranged villain who'd imprisoned his parents and dragged him back through time in the first place. True, Greg had expected to confront him tonight, but not yet. And his appearance now made for a very big problem.

Well, at least he can't hear me, Greg thought, his heart racing.

And then the rock his foot was resting on broke loose.

PART ONE

THE
LOUVRE

ONE

Three days earlier *and* four hundred years later . . .

"What's wrong, Greg? You've always wanted to visit Paris!"

Greg turned from the cab window and frowned at his cheerful mom, squished in the backseat beside him. He'd been watching the tour boats on the Seine River, crammed full of tourists gaping at the Eiffel Tower, all with equally cheerful faces.

"Yeah, but on vacation," he said.

"This *is* a vacation," his father replied.

"I guess." Greg wasn't sure. Being forced to sell all your

possessions in order to survive didn't seem to be very vacation-like. On the other hand, maybe his mom and dad *would* cash in and the three of them would all live happily ever after. That's what his parents kept repeating, over and over and over. And Greg wanted to believe it. He really did. Otherwise . . . well, it was best not to think about the alternative.

Dad reached across Mom and patted Greg's shoulder. Greg's father was built like a twig, tall and thin, with dark, wavy hair that always got messed up in the wind. "I admit, we're not here for the best reasons, but that doesn't mean we can't have some fun," he said. "Look, there's the Pont Neuf! The oldest bridge in Paris. It was built more than four hundred years ago!"

"Neat," Greg said. He meant it, but the word came out as more of a groan.

"Come on, Greg," Mom said soothingly. She had dressed to impress today, wearing her most expensive dress and her tallest heels, her blond hair so shellacked with hair spray Greg figured he could probably bounce a rock off it. "We're going to the Louvre right now! The greatest museum in the world. And *we're* getting a private tour!"

"But did we really have to sell *everything* to get it?" Greg asked quietly.

Mom and Dad sighed.

Greg turned back to the window and caught his own reflection in it. Like his parents, he was thin and pale, with thick brown curls—but he was short for fourteen, and right now his dark brown eyes looked like a sad puppy's. *Yikes.* He shifted his gaze back to the passing scenery. Around the curve of the Seine, he could see the Louvre ahead. It was impossible to miss: an ornate palace that took up several city blocks. Festooned with carvings and flourishes, it was as much a work of art as the paintings inside. It looked like a giant stone wedding cake.

"It's not like we're *giving* everything away," Greg's father chided. "We are *selling* it. And the museum is being very generous."

"I know," Greg muttered. "It's just . . . Grandpa Gus always told us we weren't supposed to sell *anything.*"

"Then maybe Grandpa Gus shouldn't have squandered so much of the family savings," Greg's mother countered.

Out the window, the setting sun turned the Seine a sparkling gold. There was no denying Paris was a beautiful city. Even in his funk, Greg could admit that. If only he could enjoy the trip and be like those tourists on the boats, but his grandfather's warning kept ringing in his ears.

These heirlooms must always stay in our family, no matter what.

Greg was ten years old when the old man had said those words, on one of his famous tours of the family's Connecticut estate. Grandpa Gus had still been living with them, before he got shipped off to a nursing home. Everyone else in the family had long ago grown bored of being dragged around the mansion on Sunday afternoons, hearing the same old tales of how the Rich family had come to acquire such magnificent treasures from around the globe. But not Greg, who adored his eccentric grandfather. However, on that particular tour, Grandpa Gus had grown uncharacteristically serious. *These things are more important than you can possibly understand*, he'd whispered. *Do whatever it takes to protect them. And most important of all . . .*

"He said we should never take them to France," Greg recalled out loud.

Dad smiled sadly. "He also said his beagle had been George Washington in a former life. The man's compass didn't exactly point due north."

There was a screech of tires behind them, followed by a cacophony of tinny French car horns. Greg spun around. The huge moving truck following them—the one stuffed with all their possessions—had just plowed through a red light, trying to keep up. Cars swerved left and right to avoid it.

"French drivers," Mom remarked with a chuckle. "They're as bad as the Italians."

But not nearly as bad as anyone in New York, Greg thought, more depressed than ever. For some reason, the truck reminded him of how much had changed for the worse in the past year, and how far his family had fallen. Recently his whole life seemed to revolve around loading and unloading trucks.

First, his parents had run out of money. Not that this was much of a surprise. For years now, Dad had made no secret that maintaining the family estate cost more than he earned. But when he finally announced, "We're broke," it still came as a shock.

After that, everything had blurred into a routine of selling and moving. So long, Connecticut—where Greg had lived his whole life, where his family had lived for generations, in fact—hello, Queens. So long, beautiful estate—with a duck pond, stables, and a fifty-room mansion—hello, cramped three-room apartment. So long, private school—hello, public.

Mom and Dad couldn't even wait until the end of ninth grade. They had to uproot Greg right in the middle of the year. Which would have been okay. Honestly. He hadn't made any truly close friends at Wellington Prep. But there was the small matter of making *new* friends. Back in Connecticut, his skills—horseback riding, fluent French, fencing (he was favored to win the tristate tournament in his age bracket)—had at least made him interesting. At Carver High, they made him a freak. (When Greg had boasted to a girl in his homeroom about his fencing skills, she'd misunderstood and tried to have him arrested for selling stolen property.)

Greg had always felt he wasn't quite like other kids his age, but now everyone at school seemed to share that feeling. On the very first day, a group of bullies had discovered he was reading *20,000 Leagues Under the Sea* in the original French. Worse, they discovered he was reading it just for fun.

They responded by stealing his lunch money and flushing it down the toilet.

Plus, the irony of being named Rich when he no longer was . . . well, even the dumbest kids could make fun of *that*.

But maybe things were turning around. After all, if the Louvre hadn't approached his parents, the "Rich" family (*Ha! Get it?* Greg thought)—well, they might have had to unload everything on eBay.

The museum's interest had come out of the blue. Greg's parents had known their furniture was antique but never expected it might be of historical value. And then they'd received a letter from Michel Dinicoeur, the museum's director of Renaissance acquisitions: *"I, Michel Dinicoeur, have discovered you possess some artifacts of great interest to the Louvre, some of which I have been trying to track down for a very long time. . . ."*

After that, arrangements were made quickly. The museum even footed the bill for plane tickets, the hotel, and shipping everything to France. Greg had hoped the trip would cheer him up, but from the moment he stepped off the plane, he'd been overwhelmed by a sense of foreboding.

His parents had done their best to rouse his spirits, pointing out the famous landmarks on the way in from the airport and enthusiastically making plans for the rest of the week. They'd just spent the afternoon at the Eiffel Tower, even splurging for lunch at the famous Jules Verne restaurant on the second deck. But Greg simply couldn't shake the feeling that Grandpa Gus had known what he was talking about—and that coming to Paris was a terrible mistake.

They passed the Tuileries—acres of formal gardens and spouting fountains—and arrived at the Louvre. The cab began to turn into the central plaza, where I. M. Pei's modern glass pyramid sat above the underground main entrance, a stark contrast to the formal old museum that surrounded it. "Sorry," Greg's father told the driver in French. "We're not tourists. We're going to the loading docks around back."

The cabdriver shrugged, then made a death-defying swerve back into traffic and continued on the road between the massive museum and the Seine.

"Everything's going to be fine, Greg," Mom said for the hundredth time. She patted Greg's knee, trying to comfort him. But Greg noticed her fingering the silver chain around her neck, something she always did when she was nervous or upset. Her nails absently tapped the black crystal that hung from it.

Greg had never seen his mom without the crystal, even when she exercised. It wasn't a precious stone, and it wasn't even intact—one side was jagged, as though half of it had broken off—but it *was* beautiful and otherworldly. When he was younger, Greg had imagined it might have been a meteorite cast off by a passing comet. Grandpa Gus said it had been in the family going all the way back to their distant ancestor, Cardinal Richelieu, who had been adviser to the kings of France four hundred years ago. But as with everything Gus said, nobody—including Mom herself—seemed to take him seriously. Still, she loved it. Greg's dad had given it to her when he proposed. At least Greg could be certain they wouldn't sell *that* off, and in the midst of his internal upheaval he felt comforted.

The cab rounded the corner of the museum and stopped by a gate where armed guards stood.

The driver turned back to Greg's father, unsure what to do.

Mr. Rich dug into his pocket and pulled at another piece of correspondence from Michel Dinicoeur—including directions and a silver pass. He rolled down the window and handed it to the stone-faced guard along with the passports of everyone in the family. The guard stepped into a booth, made a phone call to his superior, then returned the passports and raised the gate, waving them through. The cab and the truck plunged down a ramp that led underneath the museum. Greg felt as though he was being swallowed by the earth.

"Isn't this exciting?" his mother asked. "More than eight million people a year visit this museum, and almost none of them get to see this."

"Wow," Greg said, joking. "The loading dock. This is *way* better than the *Mona Lisa*."

"Greg, that's enough," his father said with a tired sigh. "All those years of private school and French tutors and the lessons for horseback riding and fencing and rock climbing . . . They weren't *free*, you know. I don't remember you complaining then."

Greg frowned, ashamed. His father was right. On the other hand, while Greg might have spent some of the family money, he hadn't *lost* any of it. The Riches had been slowly squandering their fortune for over a century, splurging on lousy art and racehorses with bad knees. Even Grandpa Gus was guilty of it.

It didn't really bother Greg that there would be nothing left to inherit. He wasn't *that* spoiled or selfish. What bothered him was that with all the drastic changes in his life, he felt upended, rootless. As though the person he was before no longer existed, or didn't matter. So far he hadn't been able to forge his way into the new life. Would he ever be able to?

The loading area was warm and humid and stank of exhaust fumes. As the cab slowed to a stop, a strange man emerged from the bowels of the museum. Greg's eyes narrowed. At first, he wasn't sure if he wanted to laugh or . . . *what*. The man was around thirty, tall and broad-shouldered—with long black hair, a thin mustache, and a small, pointed beard. His clothing wasn't just striking, it was ridiculous. Instead of a suit, he wore breeches, stockings, and a loose-fitting shirt. Greg thought he looked more like an actor on his way to perform Shakespeare than a museum employee. Maybe the people who worked here had to dress up in costume?

"I, Michel Dinicoeur, am pleased to make your acquaintance!" the man cried. He pronounced his own name with an overly dramatic flourish, stressing each syllable as though it was in italics: *Me-shell Di-ni-coo-rre*. "Welcome to the Louvre!"

TWO

THIS *DEFINITELY* DIDN'T FEEL LIKE VACATION.

Greg doubted he could have imagined something more unpleasant to do in Paris than stand on a broiling loading dock, watching strange workmen unload his family's belongings. Even the opera would have been better. At least the opera was air-conditioned.

On the other hand, Michel Dinicoeur appeared to be having the time of his life. He flitted about, oohing and ahhing over each piece of furniture with delight. "These are exquisite!" he gushed about the dining room chairs, then shot Greg's mother a sly glance. "Almost as beautiful as you, Mrs. Rich."

Greg's mother laughed and blushed. "Oh, Mr. Dinicoeur. You're a charmer."

Really? Greg thought. He stood on his tiptoes, leaning up to his father's ear. "Does this guy seem slimy to you?" he whispered.

"Oh, he's not slimy," his father replied. "He's just French."

As far as Mom and Dad were concerned, Michel Dinicoeur could do no wrong. They both gasped in awe at his knowledge of antiques and laughed every time he said something creepy. Greg couldn't tell if they really thought Dinicoeur was charming—or if they were just sucking up to him because he'd swung them a free trip to France and was saving their bank account. Whatever the reason, Greg had no stomach for it. He wandered off to the side of the loading dock, watching his family's belongings vanish . . . Correction: They weren't his family's belongings. Not anymore. Now they were the museum's.

Suddenly Dinicoeur sniffed in disgust.

Greg's massive desk had just come off the truck. Before it was Greg's, Grandpa Gus had used it as boy, and he'd claimed that it had belonged to *his* grandfather. It was sturdy and ornate, hewn from oak. Greg knew why they had to get rid of it, and it wasn't for the money. There was no place for it in their cramped apartment; it couldn't even fit through the door.

"What is *that*?" Dinicoeur asked with a sneer.

"Just an old desk," Greg's mother said apologetically, as if she was embarrassed to have brought it. "We know it's not of the same period as everything else, but . . . We thought you wanted *everything*."

Dinicoeur clucked his tongue. "Being old doesn't make something an antique. Though I suppose we can find a place for it in our offices." He waved it aside dismissively. The workmen dutifully set it on the dock near Greg, far from the rest of the heirlooms, as if it carried a disease they might catch.

For Greg's whole life, the desk had been placed against the wall of his room. He'd never seen the back of it until now. To his surprise it was covered with intricate carvings. Perhaps it had been a businessman's desk, and the back was supposed to face and impress clients. Greg instantly recognized fleurs-de-lis, the famous emblems of French royalty. There were a dozen emblazoned on raised circles . . . though one was tilted to the side, as if it were a knob. . . .

Without thinking, Greg reached out and twisted it. The fleur-de-lis rotated easily. Greg heard a click, and then the thump of something dropping inside the top drawer. Greg scurried around to the other side of the desk and yanked the drawer open. He'd cleaned out the desk before they'd moved—but now, nestled in the back of the drawer, he saw a small book, bound in leather with a strap knotted around it.

The pages were brown and the cover was coated in a thin layer of dust. Greg wiped off the book on his shorts and found four words embossed on the leather:

Property of Jacob Rich

Greg's eyes widened in surprise. Jacob was Gus's grandfather, Greg's great-great-grandfather. Intrigued, Greg opened the book. The spine was stiff with age and the pages coughed up clouds of dust. They were filled with neat rows of Jacob's crisp, concise handwriting, vestiges of a time when people wrote actual letters rather than text messages. At the top of the first page was a brief introduction:

> 4/7
> *In any life, there comes a time for introspection. This is my time. Or more importantly, to detail what I know. Here now, perhaps more than ever, it is important that pen meets paper. This is the task I will undertake for thine eyes.*

"You must be Gregory."

Startled, Greg palmed the diary and whirled around to find Michel Dinicoeur looming over him. "Greg," he corrected.

"Sorry I've been so distracted since you arrived, but I wanted to say hello." Dinicoeur extended his right hand.

Greg shook it—and flinched. Dinicoeur's hand felt cold and inhuman. He glanced at it. It wasn't real. Instead, it was an amazingly lifelike prosthesis. Greg had never touched a fake hand before. He recoiled, snapping his own hand away before he was even aware of what he was doing. His face flushed. "Um—sorry—"

"Greg!" his mother scolded.

"No, it's my fault." Dinicoeur smiled. "I should have warned him. I've had it so long, I forget about it sometimes."

"What happened to it?" Greg asked.

Dinicoeur laughed good-naturedly. "I made a mistake long ago. I simply wasn't careful. But I've learned my lesson. Were you doing something with the desk, Greg?"

"Just saying good-bye to it." Greg patted the scarred wood top.

Dinicoeur studied him carefully . . . until a loud *bang* diverted his attention. One of the workmen had dropped a chest of drawers. Dinicoeur cursed under his breath and ran back down the loading dock. "Careful with that! It's worth more than you'll earn in ten years!"

Greg took advantage of the distraction. The diary was just small enough to fit in one of the large pockets of his cargos. He was dying to read more of it, but not while

Dinicoeur was on the prowl. There'd be plenty of time later, back at the hotel.

"I hate to sound picky," Dinicoeur announced to Greg's parents. "But we did discuss one piece that *wasn't* furniture. . . ."

"It's right here," Greg's mother said, pointing to her necklace, which was now concealed beneath her shirt. "Sorry. I couldn't resist wearing it one last time."

Dinicoeur's eyes lit up, glittering like the crystal itself. "I understand completely. Well, we've spent more than enough time on this horrid dock, haven't we? How would you like to see the future home of your belongings?"

Greg's jaw dropped. He couldn't believe it. Mom was giving up her necklace too?

But his parents were beside themselves with excitement. Night was falling and the Louvre had closed, meaning that soon they'd be seeing some of the world's greatest works of art without fighting the crowds like everyone else.

Dinicoeur led the way. The loading dock was on the basement level, which opened into a long hallway flanked by massive, climate-controlled art storage rooms with thick steel doors and coded keypad entries. Dinicoeur swiftly ushered them through the passage and into the museum itself. To Greg's amazement, the first thing he saw was a huge stone wall with rounded turrets at each end—as if part of an ancient castle sat in the basement of the museum.

Dinicoeur chuckled. "This is the medieval Louvre," he explained. "This building has been many things throughout its history, though it began as a fortress. Eight centuries ago, when Paris was a walled city, this building guarded the main entrance. But when the city expanded beyond the walls in the 1500s, the Louvre became useless as a defense. So it became the royal palace, home to the king and queen of France for over two hundred years."

For a moment, Greg forgot his worries. "Wow. I didn't know that."

"It's true," Dinicoeur said. "In fact, I suspect many of the items you've brought back with you used to be in the palace. Now, after four centuries, they have finally returned home!"

"Isn't that exciting?" Greg's mother asked. "I always suspected they were special! Imagine, Greg. King Louis XIII might have sat on one of our chairs!"

"I can practically guarantee it," Dinicoeur said with a sly smile.

Over the next hour, he escorted the Rich family through the vast, ornate halls, pointing out everything of interest along the way. Except for the security guards who patrolled in teams, the foursome had the entire museum to themselves. They made their way up massive stone staircases and through gigantic galleries, past Greek antiquities, Egyptian artifacts, and medieval art . . . until they finally arrived in a grand room filled with paintings of Paris four hundred years before.

"This was one of the staterooms of Henry IV, the father of Louis XIII," Dinicoeur began. "Both kings were instrumental in turning the Louvre from a medieval fortress into the great building it is today." He waved around the room at its beautifully decorated walls, the inlaid wooden floor, and a soaring ceiling painted full of fat cherubs and clouds. "The royal family lived here during the reconstruction, but then, they *had* to. It took over fifty years to renovate this entire building. But it was worth it. Here's what this very room looked like back before it was redone." He pointed to a painting so large that it stretched almost from the ceiling to the floor, portraying a dark, dismal room decorated with dreary tapestries. The only furnishing was a large, spindly-looking chair.

"What is that?" Greg's father asked.

"The king's throne," Dinicoeur replied.

"*That* was the throne?" Mom cried. "It looks like it came from IKEA!"

Greg laughed in spite of himself, glancing around. "I can't believe this is the same place. When was that picture painted?"

"In 1615, five years into the reign of Louis XIII," Dinicoeur replied. "Have you studied French history at school?"

"Not much," Greg admitted.

The truth was, even at Wellington Prep, they'd focused a lot on American history, but not much on the rest of the world. All of European history had been crammed into two semesters, and he'd missed most of the last part when he'd transferred schools. He didn't know squat about the major players in French history except for Napoleon.

"Such a shame," Dinicoeur said with a sigh. "France has a magnificent history, filled with great men, great wars, and—"

"Great Scott," said Greg's mother, peering into the next room. "This is incredible."

"Ah, yes," said the Frenchman. "The crown jewels."

Greg followed the three adults through the archway and gasped. Behind thick protective glass sat the property of kings: crowns, tiaras, pendants, and scepters, all forged from gold and silver and encrusted with precious stones. Diamonds, emeralds, rubies, and sapphires gleamed. Greg's eyes roved over swords and daggers with gem-covered hilts.

Dinicoeur turned to Greg's mother. Greg noticed him lick his lips. "Shall we return *your* necklace to its rightful place here?"

Greg's mother's hand reflexively went to her crystal. "You mean . . . *this* was one of the crown jewels?" she gasped.

Dinicoeur laughed. "Well, no. That crystal isn't precious. But the piece does date back to the time of the Bourbon kings. It doesn't belong in *this* room, but it will be a wonderful addition to our collection." He extended his hand.

Greg held his breath. *Please, Mom. Don't do it. Not that . . .*

To his surprise and relief, his mother stepped back. Her hand closed around the crystal protectively. "I'm sorry, Mr. Dinicoeur. I've changed my mind about this one. It's too special to me. . . ."

Anger flashed in Dinicoeur's eyes. Only for a second, but it was there.

Greg looked to his parents. His father put his arm around his mother protectively.

"Mrs. Rich," Dinicoeur began. He was trying hard to sound calm, but Greg could hear frustration seeping into his voice. "We had a deal."

"I know," Greg's mother said. "And I'll be happy to refund the money to you. You can have all the other pieces. Just not this one."

"But that's the one I need!" Dinicoeur shouted. He lunged at Greg's mother.

She shrieked and tried to slip away, but the Frenchman moved with surprising speed, knocking Greg's father out of the way. Dinicoeur's hand closed around the crystal and, with one powerful jerk, he snapped the chain that held it.

At the same time, he shoved Greg's mother backward into the display case that held the ceremonial crowns.

Alarms blared.

And with that, Dinicoeur bolted from the room, the crystal in his hand.

THREE

It took a moment for Greg to process what was happening. Dinicoeur had escaped. Red lights were flashing. A piercing siren filled the air. Far more troubling, a metal security wall had started to drop in the doorway, threatening to seal his family inside the exhibition gallery.

Greg spotted a small wooden stool, presumably left for the museum guards. Without thinking, he snatched it and shoved it under the descending steel slab. It struck the stool, splintering the wood and buckling the legs. But miraculously the stool held. A narrow gap remained between the wall and the floor.

"Hurry!" Greg cried over the alarm. He ushered his parents toward the doorway.

Neither Dad nor Mom protested. They fell to the floor and slithered out of the chamber. Greg went last. Barely a second after he was through, the stool collapsed and the wall came crashing down.

Dinicoeur stood in front of the massive painting of the pre-restored room. He removed something shiny from his pocket, and Greg saw a jagged black glint in the flashing alarm lights. For a moment, Greg thought it was his mother's crystal—until he noticed Dinicoeur already held his mother's crystal in his other hand; the silver chain still dangled from it. *It's the other half!* Greg thought. He raced toward Dinicoeur—just as the Frenchman fit both pieces of the crystal together.

There was a blinding flash of light, and a powerful wave of energy rippled through the air like an invisible tsunami. Greg was blown off his feet and tumbled backward into the wall.

For a moment he lay still, rubbing his aching head. When he stood up again, he wondered if he'd banged his head and was hallucinating.

Dinicoeur had focused the crystal's light on the huge painting of the old throne room . . . and in response the painting was starting to ripple. It was far more vivid, somehow, as if it had come to life.

"Arrêtez!" Greg's father barked.

He was already on his feet, filled with a determination Greg had never seen in him. He charged, tackling the Frenchman. Both pieces of the crystal toppled from Dinicoeur's grasp, skittering across the floor. The men tumbled into the painting. To Greg's astonishment, the wavering canvas didn't rip. Instead, his father and Dinicoeur seemed to have been swallowed by the painting itself.

Greg's mom chased after them, reaching for his dad's hand. Greg saw her fall forward behind her husband, into the painted throne room.

Deep down inside, Greg figured his eyes were playing tricks on him. There had to be a rational explanation for all this. Perhaps the painting wasn't really a painting at all, but an incredible trompe l'oeil illusion, a hole in the wall that led to another gallery of the museum. And so he leaped through the frame into the throne room as well.

A wave of energy surged through him . . . and everything changed.

The rippling ceased. So did the flashing red lights. And the wail of the alarm siren.

But what really stood out was the smell.

Wherever Greg was, it *stank*. The room reeked of old wood and burned oil and a distant tang of raw sewage. It was hot, too. Nasty hot.

Greg wiped his brow, blinking the sweat out of his eyes in the dim flicker of oil lamps. He spun around, trying to make sense of it all. The frame through which he and his family and Dinicoeur had just passed shimmered with an image of the Louvre gallery—and then it winked out of existence. There was only a bare wall where it had been.

Greg rubbed his eyes. His pulse quickened. He turned to his parents, who staggered to their feet, gaping in shock.

Dinicoeur glared at the three of them. "Fools!" he barked. "You should have stayed on the other side!"

"What do you mean?" Greg's father demanded. "What's going on?"

Before Dinicoeur could answer, four soldiers raced into the room. Each wore a blue tunic emblazoned with a cross. Each carried a sword. Their dark hair was matted and stringy. Greg stared at them in astonishment. The soldiers stared back, coming to a halt. When they noticed Dinicoeur, however, they gave a gasp of recognition. They knelt before him, bowing their heads in submission.

Without missing a beat, Dinicoeur spoke to them in French. Though it wasn't exactly the French Greg had studied in school. It was more nasal, and the inflection was odd, sounding a bit like the way French Cajuns spoke in Louisiana. But Greg could still understand it.

"Arrest them! They're here to assassinate the king!"

Greg's father was closest to the soldiers. The four came for him first, swords at the ready.

Greg was now sure he'd hit his head. There was no way any of this could be real.

He ran to help his parents, but his mother's scream stopped him cold in his tracks. "No, Greg! Run!"

Greg glanced at his father. There was a don't-you-dare-disobey-me look in Dad's eyes. "Go! It's the only way to help us!"

"But—," Greg started.

"Seize the boy!" Dinicoeur yelled in French.

One of the soldiers lunged for him. Greg cast one last look at his parents, and then dashed through the closest doorway with the soldier on his heels. He ran as far as he could, retracing his steps through the museum—

—but it wasn't exactly the same place. All the art was gone. The rooms were dark and cavernous, lit only by oil lamps, if they were even lit at all. The grand staircase, made of stone when Greg had climbed it before, had been replaced by wood. A huge chandelier, thirty feet across, hung suspended by a heavy chain above it, a hundred candles flickering in its sconces.

Greg skidded to a stop at the top of the rickety stairs. Five stringy-haired, tunic-wearing soldiers waited at the bottom. The soldier behind Greg ordered them to stop him. They charged up, blocking his escape.

If this is a dream, I might as well risk it all, Greg thought. He leaped off the stairs and grabbed the chandelier.

It creaked ominously with his weight. Half the candles blew out as he swung above the stairwell. Greg let go, hit the wooden floor with a thud, and somersaulted forward, leaving the guards on the stairwell behind—then started running again.

Even in his delirious condition, a part of him wanted to turn back for his parents. They'd ordered him to go, yes. But now they'd been captured . . . or worse. And if Greg had stayed, he would have been captured or worse, too. As his father had said, the only way to help them was to run. But where? Even if he escaped, he had no idea where he was or what had happened. Everything was so unreal. The crystal, the picture . . .

It has to be a dream. Of course it's a dream.

Greg ran through room after room, the wooden floors creaking under his feet, the stuffy, smelly air threatening to suffocate him. The building was endless, with no sign of an exit anywhere. He could hear the soldiers pounding along in pursuit—and thought he heard whinnying through the floor below. Was there a stable directly beneath him?

A window appeared ahead, open wide. A soothing breeze caressed Greg's hot face. He stumbled as he ran the last few paces and peered outside, his lungs heaving, assessing the distance to the ground. It was only ten feet—high enough to prevent enemies from climbing in, but not to prevent him from leaping out, if he was careful.

Then Greg looked up, toward Paris. His throat caught.

The city was gone.

The jammed streets, the tour boats, the cacophony of taxi horns and ambulance sirens . . . the jumbled topography of church spires, domed monuments, and skyscrapers, all overshadowed by the Eiffel Tower . . . All of it had been replaced, except for Notre Dame, which now towered over everything else. The Seine was dark and untamed. Few of the buildings stood over two stories. The stagnant air was so quiet that Greg could hear the sound of horses' hooves and conversations on the other side of the river, but it was thick with that powerful odor: horse dung and sweat and sewage. He glanced up at the night sky. The narrow streets were lit only by the weak glow of candles and oil lamps from within houses, and without the light pollution of a million neon signs and every other kind of electrical power source, Greg could see more stars than he ever had in his life.

It wasn't a dream. It couldn't be. It felt too real.

He'd gone back in time.

PART TWO

PARIS, 1615

FOUR

GREG WASN'T SURE HOW MUCH TIME HAD PASSED SINCE he'd jumped out the window onto the narrow dirt road that ran between the Louvre and the Seine—a road pocked with mud puddles and steaming piles of horse manure. Fear made it impossible to gauge time. All he knew for sure was that he was running into this strange version of Paris, rather than away from it. He *couldn't* run away from it. The entire city was surrounded by a wall. A massive, three-story stone wall with armed guards patrolling the top of it.

There were gates, of course, but there were even more guards stationed at those. A huge gate blocked the road just west of the Louvre. From the size, Greg guessed it was the main entrance into Paris. He could see the guards positioned in the towers on each side of it, on the lookout for enemies.

He couldn't risk getting caught. The guards at the Louvre thought he'd been sent to assassinate the king.

So Greg had turned and headed in the opposite direction, deeper into Paris. *This is totally insane.* He didn't even know if he could get along alone in *modern* Paris, let alone the medieval version of it. How was he ever going to survive?

The shadowy city streets beyond the palace were empty, but even in the dim torchlight Greg could see that the homes were surprisingly small and filthy. Garbage was strewn everywhere. A housewife tossed the remains of dinner out her window as Greg ran past, nearly hitting him in the face with a bowlful of gruel and bones. Two rats the size of small dogs streaked past him and fell upon the remains.

As disgusting as the rats were, the Seine was worse. The stench nearly made Greg gag. Gutters ran straight from the houses into the water, as if the river were one big sewer. Clouds of flies hovered along the banks.

Greg tried to catch his breath without breathing through his nose. *Who is Michel Dinicoeur?* he wondered. The Frenchman was the key to all of this. It seemed everything he'd arranged—the trip to Paris, the offer to buy the family heirlooms—all of it had merely been a ruse to get his hands on the crystal. Was he a real employee of the Louvre, then? If not, how had he managed to infiltrate the museum? And how had the soldiers in *this* palace known him?

Shivering despite the warm air, Greg spotted a bridge upriver, slicing across the western tip of the Île de la Cité: the island in the center of Paris. Greg knew from the bridge's location that it was the Pont Neuf; he'd seen it earlier, from the taxi. It looked almost the same as it had in the future, only far newer. Without cars on it, it was a surprisingly wide promenade. Best of all, Greg could see people. If the soldiers were still after him, he could lose himself in the crowd for a few minutes and buy some time to think. He made his way onto the bridge.

Unfortunately, the crowd smelled worse than the river. As far as Greg could tell, everyone who lived in this version of Paris was a derelict or a drunk. They reeked of body odor, bad breath, and alcohol. All sported clothes similar to those Dinicoeur had worn: loose shirts and tight stockings. Everyone's hair was parted straight down the middle. (Maybe parting on the side hadn't been invented yet?) But given how they stared at him, Greg knew he must have looked a lot weirder to *them* in his T-shirt, shorts, and sneakers.

His head down, Greg ducked and dodged through the sea of puzzled faces. Behind him, he could hear angry shouting: the soldiers *were* after him, drawing close now, bulldozing through the mob. Greg had intended to cross to the other side of the river, but two more soldiers raced onto the bridge from the far bank. His heart caught. Those soldiers would spot him in seconds. Now, the only way to escape was onto the Île de la Cité itself. He veered off the bridge where it met the tip of the island and into a maze of alleys.

His knees ached. He needed to find someplace safe to hide and rest. Someplace he could ask for protection . . .

And then he saw it, straight ahead of him: Notre Dame.

The cathedral was about the only thing in Paris that looked *exactly* the same as it would centuries later—only now it loomed above every other building on the island, the tallest structure in the city. Greg wound through the alleys until he reached its massive front doors and pushed on the heavy wood with all his might. They were locked. He pounded on them, but his fists hardly made a sound. Yelling for help was out of the question. It would only alert the soldiers. Summoning what little strength he had left, he ducked along the building, searching for another way in.

Aha. There was a walled-off courtyard behind the church, the stones rough and pitted. Greg had done plenty of rock climbing. This was a piece of cake. He scrambled over the top and dropped into a garden. All at once, his nostrils relaxed. It smelled . . . well, *good* here. Like the produce aisle in a high-end grocery store. He was surrounded by fruit trees and vegetables: a patch of green in the midst of the squalid city. Greg slipped through a tangle of melon vines, passing a scarecrow on his way to the back door—

The scarecrow suddenly came to life.

It pounced on Greg, flattening him in a patch of rosemary. A hand covered Greg's mouth before he could scream. The other tightly clutched his neck.

"The church does not look kindly upon thieves," the attacker hissed, pressing his knees into Greg's chest.

Greg squinted at him, struggling to breathe. To his surprise, he found himself staring at a boy not much older than him—with long brown hair, a thin nose, and piercing blue eyes. He wasn't much taller than Greg but was clearly strong. He wore a brown cloak over breeches and a shirt that looked as if they had been torn and stitched a thousand times.

"I wasn't stealing!" Greg protested in French. "I'm looking for . . ." He struggled to come up with the right word, knowing there was a medieval term for a holy place that provided immunity from the law. "Sanctuary!"

The older boy's brow furrowed in confusion, as though he was having trouble understanding Greg's French. He removed his hand from Greg's mouth, but kept the other on his neck. "You wish for sanctuary?"

"Yes," Greg gasped.

The boy took a closer look at Greg's T-shirt and shorts.

"You speak and dress very strangely," he said. "Where are you from?"

Greg suddenly remembered a long-ago lecture in French class, back at Wellington Prep. According to his teacher, the language had changed so much over time that people a few centuries before would have trouble understanding modern French. Plus, in the past, there had been such great differences in the regional dialects of France itself that people from different parts of the country had difficulty communicating.

"Far away," Greg answered. He presumed that was as much of the truth as anyone could handle.

"And you have come all the way to Paris for sanctuary?" the boy asked skeptically.

"Er . . . no. Not exactly. I wasn't, uh . . . accused of the crime until I got here."

"What crime?"

Before Greg could answer, someone banged on the garden gate. "Open up! This is Captain Valois of the king's guard! We seek a boy who has tried to assassinate the king!"

The boy's grip tightened on Greg's neck. "You're an assassin?"

"No," Greg whispered urgently. "I've been wrongly accused—"

Another loud clang cut him off. "Open this gate now, by order of the king!" Valois barked.

"Hold on! I'm coming!" The boy stood and withdrew a thin rapier from beneath his cloak, although he almost seemed embarrassed to reveal it. "If you try to escape, I will kill you," he warned.

"This is a mistake," Greg pleaded. "Please! I didn't do anything—"

"Enough." The boy pressed the tip of his sword against Greg's neck. "Do not move. Do not utter another sound."

Greg held his breath and watched through the rosemary as the boy went and opened the gate. Four soldiers stood outside, wielding torches. Their light spilled into the garden. Greg stayed as still as he could, hoping to blend into the shadows.

"There is no assassin here," the boy told the soldiers.

"Stand aside. We shall see for ourselves." Valois, the captain, was a mountain of a man with beady eyes and a mustache as thick as a sausage. He tried to force the gate open farther to storm through, but to his surprise—and Greg's—the boy held it firm.

"You have no right," the boy said calmly.

"We have an order from the palace!" Valois roared.

"This is church land," the boy countered. "The palace has no rule over it."

"Step aside, boy!"

The boy shook his head, but even from his hiding place, Greg could hear him swallow. "If you really seek an assassin, then he's escaping while you waste your time here. Do you want to catch him . . . or do you wish to provoke the anger of the church against the throne?"

Valois glared at the boy but finally stepped back. "Your insolence will not be forgotten," he spat, then whirled and disappeared into the night, the other soldiers following.

Pent-up air burst from Greg's burning lungs. "Thank you," he croaked when the boy returned.

"Don't thank me yet." The boy aimed his rapier at Greg again. "You have much to answer, and I can still turn you over to them. Now tell me, how did you earn the wrath of the king's guard?"

"I didn't try to assassinate the king."

"So you've said. But I would have guessed anyway. How old are you, fourteen?"

"Yes."

"I'm not aware of many fourteen-year-old assassins. What happened?"

Greg thought for a moment, knowing that the full story might earn him a trip to whatever the medieval equivalent of an insane asylum was. Or, given that he was at a church, maybe the boy would think he'd been possessed. "A man took something that belonged to my parents," he answered carefully. "When we followed him to the palace to get it back, he told the soldiers we were there to assassinate the king."

The boy eyed Greg for a moment. "And who was this man?"

"Michel Dinicoeur."

The boy frowned. "I've never heard of him."

"The soldiers knew him. He has long hair and a pointed beard. . . ."

"That could be virtually anyone in the king's guard."

"He's missing his right hand."

The boy's eyebrows rose, but he still shook his head. "Sorry, I don't really know the names of anyone who serves the king."

Really? Greg thought. The palace was close by—and it was the most important place in France. Greg knew plenty about the White House and the people who worked there, and that was over two hundred miles from where he lived. . . . But then Greg realized he was still thinking like someone from the twenty-first century. What happened in the White House was constantly covered on the internet and twenty-four-hour news channels. But here . . . had newspapers even been invented yet? How *did* anyone learn anything about the palace or the king? The only way would be by word of mouth, which would probably end up more rumor than fact.

"Well, whoever Dinicoeur is, he has my parents," Greg said. The terrible thought that had been haunting him burst out of his mouth. "You don't think he—"

"Killed them?" the boy finished. "I doubt it. Only the

king has the authority to demand an execution on the spot. But I fear the alternative may not be much better for them. Enemies of the crown are sent to La Mort Triste."

Greg translated the phrase in his head. *The Sad Death*. "What is that?"

"The worst prison in Paris. Even if you're not scheduled for execution, you don't survive long. It's a disease pit."

Greg's father's last words echoed in his head: *Go! It's the only way to help us!*

"I have to get them out of there," Greg said.

The boy held up a hand. "There's nothing you can do for them at this hour. Come inside and rest. You've had a difficult night."

Greg's first thought was that his parents weren't getting any rest if they were inside La Mort Triste, but the boy was right. He was starving and exhausted. "Thank you," he said. "It's very kind of you to help me when you've only just met me."

"You've come to Notre Dame for sanctuary," the boy replied. "By our code it is my duty to help the helpless. And, no offense, but you seem extremely helpless at the moment." He smiled to soften his words.

Greg smiled back. "What's your name?" he asked.

"Aramis."

For some reason, the name sounded familiar, though

Greg couldn't place it. "Thank you, Aramis. I'm Greg."

"Greg?" Aramis laughed, and then caught himself. "I beg your forgiveness. That was rude of me. But *Greg* is the strangest name I've ever heard."

FIVE

FIVE MINUTES LATER, GREG FOUND HIMSELF IN A TINY garret tucked under the roof at the rear of Notre Dame. Given that the cathedral was a beautiful gem of a building, Greg had expected every room to match the exterior. However, Aramis's room was a dump. The roof pitched steeply above and wind whistled through gaps in the stone wall. There was only one tiny window. Despite the breeze, the room was stifling, having spent the day cooking in the summer sun.

Aramis had only two candles, which didn't provide great

light, but there wasn't much to see: only a rickety stool and a small desk that sagged under the weight of thick, poorly made books. There was no bed; only some ratty blankets spread over a thatch of straw. Still, Greg was grateful for it. It certainly beat being back on the street, running for his life.

As Greg leaned back into the straw, something in his pocket dug into his leg: his great-great-grandfather's diary. He'd forgotten all about it since tucking it away.

Greg blinked wearily. Being on that loading dock seemed like days ago, when it was only an hour before he'd wound up here . . . or centuries *after*, depending on how he thought about it. But this wasn't the time to see what Jacob Rich had written. There were plenty of questions he needed answers to first.

"I—well, um, I know this will sound crazy, but . . . could you tell me what year it is?" Greg stammered.

Aramis laughed. "Why, 1615, of course! Were you struck on the head as you fled the soldiers?"

1615! Greg did his best to hide his astonishment and tried to change the subject. "How is it that you live here in the cathedral? Are you studying to be a priest?"

"A priest?" Aramis laughed again. "Do I look like nobility to you?"

"I—I suppose not."

"My parents make and sell cloth in Paris. My older brother will inherit their business, so they bought me a position as a cleric here at our church."

"What's that?"

Aramis looked askance at Greg, as though wondering how anyone could be so ignorant. "You don't know what a cleric does?"

"We don't have clerics where I come from."

"You must not have many books then." Aramis pointed to the stack on his desk. "I translate those. Mostly from Latin to French, but sometimes from German and Hebrew as well."

"You can speak all those languages?"

"The one benefit to being a cleric is you get to learn a lot. And the room has a good view of the city . . . if you don't mind the leaking roof, the heat, the rats, or the bats."

"Do all clerics carry swords?"

Aramis looked away, as though ashamed. "No. We're not supposed to. But in this city, it never hurts to be prepared for anything."

"Is that what you were doing in the garden? Practicing?"

"No. I was . . . well . . . looking for something."

"What?"

Aramis leaned forward, barely speaking above a whisper. "Have you ever heard of Galileo Galilei?"

"Of course. He's the guy who discovered that the earth orbits the sun—"

"What?" Aramis stared at Greg in shock. "You believe that? That the sun is the center of the universe? Even though the church condemns Galileo and his teachings?"

Greg winced, fearing he'd made a big mistake. "Well . . . What do *you* believe?"

Aramis paused. "I don't know," he finally admitted, sounding sheepish. "The idea that God didn't put our earth at the center of everything seems so wrong, and yet . . . My eyes indicate Galileo was right." He pulled something else from the folds of his cloak: a rudimentary telescope, a simple brass tube with a polished glass lens at each end.

"Did you make that?" Greg asked.

"No, a friend did. I've been looking at the planets every night for a month, and everything Galileo said was true. Saturn *does* have rings. And there are definitely moons orbiting Jupiter. Have you ever seen them?"

"Sure. We used to have a telescope at our house. You could even see Uranus with it."

"What's Uranus?"

"The seventh planet . . ." The words had tumbled out of Greg's mouth before he could catch himself.

"Seventh planet?" Aramis frowned once again. "There are only seven: Mercury, Venus, Earth, Mars, Jupiter, Saturn, and the moon."

Greg just nodded. Best to keep his mouth shut, or when he did have to speak, to agree with everything this kid said. "You're right," he said. "I misspoke. I'm exhausted. It's been a long day."

Aramis stared at him for a long while and then broke into

a genuine smile. "You're a very strange person."

"Not where I come from," Greg replied defensively, even though that wasn't quite true. Every kid in twenty-first-century Queens thought he was a weirdo, too.

"Wherever that is," Aramis said with a good-natured smirk. "Very far away, I suspect. You have no clerics, but you do have an extra planet. I've never seen clothes like yours before. Especially your shoes. What on earth is this substance?" He prodded the sole of Greg's sneaker.

"Rubber."

"Fascinating. And what are these slits in your clothing?"

Greg had to laugh. "You've never seen pockets before?"

"No. What are they for?"

"To keep things in. Like keys and money."

"You mean, instead of a purse?"

"Yes." Greg bit his lip. They didn't even have *pockets* in 1615?

Thankfully, Aramis didn't seem suspicious as much as intrigued. He caught Greg's wrist and gazed at his watch as if it were a priceless jewel. "And *this*. This is the most fascinating of all. A miniature clock that fits on your wrist! You must have the most incredible craftsmen in your town."

Greg suppressed another laugh. He'd bought it at Target for $19.99.

"I have heard they have great craftsmen in the Artagnan region, but that the people there have very different customs from us. Is that where you're from?"

"It is," Greg answered, even though he hadn't the faintest idea of where Artagnan was. It was better than the truth.

"Ha!" Aramis beamed, pleased with his deduction. "I've never met anyone from so far away before! Why, that's practically in Spain!"

"Yes," Greg agreed, although this was news to him.

"Well, D'Artagnan, tell me about where you're from—"

"What'd you just call me?"

"D'Artagnan. Meaning 'From Artagnan,' of course. I can't call you 'Greg.' That's simply too strange. It'll draw attention."

Greg's mind whirled. *That name!* He knew it. It suddenly clicked why the name Aramis sounded familiar, too. They were characters in *The Three Musketeers*. He'd read it in French class the year before. Aramis, Porthos, and Athos were the names of the heroes. But the main character was a newcomer named D'Artagnan. Greg also remembered that the author, Alexandre Dumas, had claimed in the preface that the characters were all based on real people in spite of how he'd made up the story. . . .

Now that Greg had been labeled D'Artagnan, his heart leaped. What if the boy before him was *the* Aramis? If so, he would eventually be renowned as one of the greatest warriors in French history. He was certainly smart. And while he claimed that he wasn't skilled with his rapier, maybe he was only being modest. Greg's parents were apparently stuck in some godforsaken prison—nearly four hundred years away from their own time—and Greg was too lost in this society to even *think* about freeing them alone. But a future musketeer would be exactly the type of person who could help him. And if he'd found Aramis, maybe the other two might be around as well. . . .

"You don't have any friends named Porthos and Athos, do you?" Greg asked.

Aramis looked at him curiously for about the thousandth time that night. "No. Why do you ask?"

"I'd heard of two great warriors by those names. And I could use all the help I can get to free my parents."

Aramis grew dour. "You have my help, D'Artagnan. But to free your parents from La Mort Triste, you're going to need much more than warriors. You're going to need the grace of God. And some stockings." He reached under the straw and tossed Greg a pair of what looked like pantyhose.

Greg frowned. There was no use protesting. But he couldn't help thinking, *Stockings? What on earth am I going to need those for?*

SIX

FLEAS. THAT WAS WHAT THE STOCKINGS WERE FOR. *Fleas.*

In the short time it took to prepare for bed, Greg discovered many annoying and disgusting things about the seventeenth century. The lack of indoor plumbing, for one. Aramis had proudly told him Notre Dame had one of the finest "privies" in the world. Upon seeing it, Greg realized this meant the rest of the world's plumbing was in very sorry shape. The toilet—which was all the way at the far end of the cathedral from Aramis's room—was nothing more than a wooden seat suspended over a foul-smelling chute that dumped its mess directly into the Seine. Plus, the seat gave splinters. Then there was no toothpaste, or soap, or washcloths. . . . And not only was the bed merely a small thatch of hay, but Aramis expected to share it with him; there was nowhere else to sleep. Greg could hear rats scurrying through the walls, and bats fluttering in and out of the belfry.

But the fleas were the worst.

Despite Aramis's warning, Greg tried to sleep without the stockings at first. Within a minute, he'd suffered a dozen bites on his legs. So he shimmied into the hot and itchy cloth, but the fleas simply migrated to other parts of his body: his arms, his torso, his neck, his ears. No bite was terribly painful, but they added up. And they didn't stop coming.

Aramis, on the other hand, was completely inured to them. He was already snoring, despite the thousands of little mites siphoning his blood.

After a while, Greg gave up. Sleep was impossible.

Though his body was tired, his mind kept racing. How was he going to rescue his parents? And even if he did pull off that feat by some miracle, how would they ever get back to their own time? Unless . . . *The crystal*. Would that work? Dinicoeur had used it to bring them here, so maybe it could bring them back. Yes, they'd left the stone in the future—in the Louvre—but if it existed then, it probably existed now, in the past too, right? Only, finding it wasn't going to be easy. In fact, it could very well be impossible. Greg didn't even know where on the entire planet to begin looking for it. Which meant he and his parents might be stuck in a world of poorly made toilet seats and ravenous bloodsucking fleas forever.

Greg glanced at his watch. It was only ten. He rarely went to sleep before midnight, although Aramis had claimed this was the latest he'd ever stayed awake. This was what life was like before the advent of electricity. Without televisions, computers, video game consoles—or even lightbulbs—life took place while the sun was up. Once it went down, there wasn't much to do except sleep. . . .

But there *was* something Greg could do. He could read Jacob Rich's diary.

Greg slunk across the creaky wooden floor and sat by the garret's single window. The half-moon had risen. Over the pitch-black nighttime city, it was surprisingly bright. A shaft of light spilled into the room, more than enough to read by. Greg emptied his pockets. In addition to the diary, he had a souvenir matchbook from his lunch at the restaurant at the Eiffel Tower, his plastic hotel card key, and a half-empty pack of gum. Oh, and forty euros' worth of money that wouldn't be minted for another four hundred years.

Last: his cell phone. *Great*, he thought dismally. A lot of good that would do him now. Back home, he couldn't go five minutes without looking at it. Here, he'd forgotten it even existed. The battery was three-quarters drained. He turned it off. For a second, he was half tempted to hurl it out the window along with the rest of his meager and use-less belongings, but he caught himself at the last second. He couldn't afford to get frustrated or freak out. Time travel might only be temporary. If he came back, he'd need the money, his phone, and his room key.

"Just read the diary," he told himself. That would distract him.

Unfortunately, after three minutes of poring over his great-great-grandfather's polished scrawl, Greg yawned. It wasn't just dull, it was the most deathly boring thing he'd ever read—the minutiae of running the family estate: how much hay had been baled for the horses, the construc-tion of a new trough for the pigs, guest lists for dinner parties full of names that didn't mean anything . . . Jacob did mention, more than once, that he was doing research into the family history and discovering "fascinating truths." But he didn't bother to share them. Eventually, even Jacob himself seemed to have grown bored. He sim-ply stopped writing, leaving over half the pages in the book blank.

Greg scowled. His great-great-grandfather went through all that trouble to hide *this*? Why? Because he was embar-rassed about how lame it was? Greg flipped back to the first lines again.

4/7

In any life, there comes a time for introspection. This is my time. Or more importantly, to detail what I know. Here now, perhaps more than ever, it is important that pen meets paper. This is the task I will undertake for thine eyes.

Now that he reread them, the lines struck him as odd. The writing was stilted, and if it was supposed to be an introduction, it raised more questions than it answered. Whose eyes did Jacob think he was writing for? And if the time had really come for introspection—or to detail what he knew—then why had he spent the whole diary writing about such uninteresting things? Maybe the boring stuff was somehow designed to camouflage something of more interest. . . .

Could it be a code?

Greg started reading with fresh eyes. But no matter how intently he studied the pages, he couldn't deduce any hidden message within them. Either there *wasn't* a code, or he didn't have the slightest idea how to find it. Another yawn escaped his lips. Well. There was only one upside to finding such a mind-numbing piece of garbage. Greg tucked it back in his pocket, sprawled on the straw beside Aramis, and—despite the fleas—fell fast asleep.

SEVEN

Greg awoke early to the sound of chirping birds, itching for a shower. Literally itching. He was so smothered with flea bites he looked like he'd been printed in Braille. Plus, he stank. And he had bits of straw jammed in places he didn't want to think about.

But of course: Showers didn't exist yet. Baths did, but the only tub was in the head priest's quarters, according to Aramis.

"Can we use it?" Greg asked hopefully.

"What for?" Aramis replied. "Do you want to get sick?"

"I want to get *clean*. I haven't bathed in almost two days."

"I haven't in over a month!" Aramis responded proudly. "Dirt blocks your pores and prevents poisonous vapors from entering your body."

"That's not true," Greg protested.

"Tell that to the king," Aramis countered. "He didn't have a single bath until he was seven and he's healthy as can be."

Greg tried to explain that back where he came from, bathing had been proven to *prevent* disease, not cause it. And furthermore, if Aramis tried it, he wouldn't smell so bad. But Aramis just laughed. "Yet another foolish belief from the backward area of Artagnan!"

Whatever. Greg could live with the stink. After all, Aramis was going out of his way to help *him*—a total stranger. He even lent Greg some clothes to help him blend in: a wool tunic that was cinched with a leather belt, soft leather shoes, and the stockings he'd slept in. The tunic was rough and chafing, but the shoes were the worst. The soles were so thin Greg could feel every stone in the floor through them. Aramis then forced him to part his curly hair down the middle. Greg had hoped to avoid this—but he changed his mind when Aramis told him his old style made him look "quite last century, from the era of Louis X." He had to blend in at all costs if he had any hope of saving his parents.

At the thought of his parents, his throat tightened. He

tried to swallow but found a lump instead. His parents were in danger. Yes, he had been angry with them. Yes, he had thought they were foolish, allowing everything they cared about to slip away. But . . . they were his parents.

"Let's you and I try to find out what happened to your family, shall we?" Aramis said gently, as if reading his mind.

Aramis planned to ask at the Hôtel de Ville if anyone had been tossed into La Mort Triste overnight. "It is a house of law for the common people of Paris," he explained, and Greg imagined it was a sort of city hall. Thankfully it wasn't far. Then again, nothing was far. Paris in 1615 was a village compared to the city it would become. The modern city Greg had left had a population of nearly twelve million people. He could only guess how many lived in this stink-pit now. Probably fewer than half a million. The entire city was a lopsided circle less than two miles across. You could walk from one end to the other in under half an hour.

Aramis donned his cleric's robe and pulled the cowl over his head.

"You probably shouldn't speak unless spoken to, D'Artagnan," he warned as they set out into the bustling streets.

Greg nodded mutely. He had no problem with that.

Once out in the sunshine, Greg could see the Louvre

in the distance, protecting the city's western gates. The Bastille protected the gates to the east; in 1615 it had yet to become a prison. The Hôtel de Ville stood directly between them, smack in the center of the city. Notre Dame, which Aramis clearly considered to be the *real* center of the city—the spiritual one—was only a few blocks south of it, just across the river.

Aramis watched Greg gape at the passersby as they snaked their way toward the bridge, and laughed. "You've never seen a city this big, have you?"

"No," Greg lied, thinking that if Aramis ever saw modern Paris, he'd die of shock.

Still, it *was* fascinating. The bridge that led to the Hôtel de Ville was lined with homes—built side to side so that you couldn't even see the water. If it weren't for the stench of the Seine, you wouldn't even know you were *on* a bridge. Aramis remarked that these were "fine places" to live, as their owners didn't have to worry about toilets at all. They just cut holes in their floors.

Just beyond the bridge on the riverbank, they came to a cramped, oddly shaped plaza: the Place de Grève, flanked by the Hôtel de Ville on the east side. Greg felt a strange flood of relief: This area existed in modern Paris, though the Place de Grève of 1615 was a lot smaller than the one he'd seen. It was also jam-packed with temporary stalls, where merchants hawked fruits and vegetables, and makeshift pens for live goats, sheep, chickens, and rabbits, while boats full of freshly caught fish lined the riverbank. Normally, Greg would have been nauseated to see live geese beheaded and eels gutted right before his eyes, but he hadn't eaten since lunch four centuries earlier, and everything made his stomach growl so loudly that Aramis could hear it.

"You must be famished," the cleric said. He pulled a small copper coin from his purse and purchased a loaf of bread still warm from the hearth.

Greg wanted to protest—Aramis had done so much for him already—but the smell of fresh bread overwhelmed him. "Thanks," he said, and dug in ravenously. He'd almost devoured the entire thing by the time they headed up the stone steps of the Hotel de Ville and through the wooden doors.

Greg glanced around warily, searching for any soldiers or guards. There didn't seem to be any. Clearly, a medieval city hall didn't need a lot of security.

"Where are we going?" he whispered.

Aramis marched purposefully up a cramped staircase to a small room on the second floor. "To see the man in charge of La Mort," he replied, then pushed open the door.

Inside the room, slumped asleep at a desk, was a boy who didn't look much older than Aramis. Greg noticed he was dressed in much nicer clothes: a bright red robe with a sash of ermine over the shoulder. "*He's* in charge of the prison?" Greg asked, dumbfounded. "I'll bet he's not even eighteen."

"So? I'm sixteen and I'm a cleric."

"Yes, but shouldn't he be doing something else?"

"Like what?" Aramis demanded.

Greg caught himself before he answered. School probably didn't even exist. There *wasn't* anything for children to do except work. Besides, how long did people even live in 1615? When the life expectancy wasn't much more than forty, eighteen must have made you middle-aged.

"I don't know how you do things in Artagnan, but here in Paris, when your family buys you an administrative job, you take what they give you," Aramis said. He rapped on the doorjamb. The boy bolted upright, startled. He didn't look all that smart, especially for someone in charge of a whole prison. A string of drool dangled from his jaw.

"What business have you here?" the boy snapped.

"I call myself Aramis, and my friend calls himself D'Artagnan," Aramis answered politely. "We have come to make a plea on behalf of the cathedral of Notre Dame. Might I ask what you call yourself?"

"Jacques Boule." The boy wiped his chin with his sleeve. "Your friend doesn't look like he works for the church."

"We are clerics there," Aramis answered cagily. "But rest assured: We are here with the full authority of the cathedral. It has come to our attention that last night, a man and a woman may have been sent to La Mort Triste from the Louvre."

"Perhaps. Let's see."

Greg shifted nervously in his uncomfortable shoes. There was only one item on Jacques's desk: a folded piece of paper, sealed with wax. As Jacques had been sleeping atop it, it was marked with a large spot of drool. He broke the seal and stared at the paper for a long while. Eventually, it occurred to Greg that he probably couldn't read. Finally, he gave up and held it out to Aramis. "You're clerics. *You* read it."

Aramis took the paper. Greg read it over his shoulder.

Let it be known to those concerned that last evening at the Louvre palace, two criminals were apprehended in an attempt to assassinate His Majesty, King Louis XIII. Both wore foreign clothing and spoke in a strange dialect. They have been incarcerated in La Mort Triste and are sentenced to death by hanging three days hence. His Majesty's Loyal Subject, Dominic Richelieu

Greg's felt his stomach plummet. He seized the door frame to steady himself.

Aramis turned to him, concerned. "These are your parents?" he whispered.

"Who else could they be?" Three days. He had only three days to save them.

"Try to remain calm. I'll see what I can do." Aramis

returned his attention to Jacques. "I beg your pardon, but we have reason to believe these two people have been improperly accused of a crime."

Jacques stiffened. "You dare accuse the Honorable Monsieur Richelieu of plotting against innocents?"

"I said no such thing," Aramis replied evenly. "We suspect that one of his less honest underlings levied this charge in order to settle a personal score."

"Accusing one of the king's guard is the same as accusing Richelieu himself," Jacques stated.

"The church doesn't see it that way," Aramis shot back. "Who can we petition for their freedom?"

Jacques shrugged. "No one. It's not possible."

Greg took a step forward, but Aramis gripped his arm. "What do you mean, 'It's not possible'?" the cleric asked. "There is no recourse at all for those unjustly accused?"

"No one in La Mort Triste is unjustly accused," Jacques said with a wicked smile. "Richelieu speaks for the king, and the king does not make mistakes."

"That's ridiculous!" Greg shouted. He couldn't help himself. "I *know* they're innocent!"

Jacques's eyes bored into Greg's. "And how do you come by this information?"

"A witness came to us at the church and told us the truth," Aramis cut in.

"And who might this witness be?" Jacques asked.

"Someone who fears retribution. She's already witnessed

two people placed in prison for something they didn't do." Aramis then faked a slight cringe, pretending to be ashamed for revealing that the supposed witness he'd just invented was a girl.

Greg held his breath. Aramis was a good liar. Would Jacques buy it?

The bureaucrat's gaze flicked from Aramis to Greg. "Every prisoner in La Mort Triste claims that they shouldn't be there. Would you have us free every one simply because someone is willing to vouch for them?"

"No," Aramis answered, "but I would expect the state to at least *listen* to dissent. To investigate claims. Otherwise, how can you be sure there are no innocents in your prison?"

"Because there aren't," Jacques stated with an edge in his voice. "No one ends up in La Mort Triste without reason."

"The people we're talking about did!" Greg blurted out.

Jacques turned to him. "Were they inside the Louvre last night?"

"They *were*, but not to assassinate the king," Greg said.

"Did they have permission to be there?" Jacques inquired.

Greg hesitated. The truth was they didn't, but how could he explain how they'd ended up in the palace without sounding insane?

Jacques sneered. "Then they were trespassing! In the palace of the king, no less. Why would anyone do that, if not for sinister reasons?"

Greg started to protest, but Aramis seized his arm again. "I think we've done all we can here. We should go."

"What?" Greg asked, aghast.

Aramis squeezed his arm tighter in response. "We should go," he hissed. *"Now."* Then he bowed to Jacques respectfully. "We're sorry for wasting your time, Monsieur Boule."

"You should be," the boy snorted. "I'm a very busy man. My time is not to be wasted." He was already laying his head back down on his desk to resume his nap before the boys had shut the door.

Aramis made a beeline for the stairs.

Greg chased after him. "What's going on?" he whispered frantically.

"Keep your voice down and read *this*." Aramis shoved the letter from Richelieu—which Jacques had apparently already forgotten about—into Greg's hand.

There was a second page under the first. The wax seal had made them stick together, so the boy hadn't noticed it at first.

There is a third assassin who remains at large. All members of the militia are advised to be on the lookout for an older boy. He will be easy to find. His skin is cleaner and whiter than most. His hair is dark and curly. His clothing is foreign, and his accent is strange.

Once apprehended, he should be brought to the office
of Dominic Richelieu at the palace of His Majesty
King Louis XIII.
God Bless the King. Long Live France!

Greg gulped in fear.

"If that idiot had been doing his job, you would have been arrested already," Aramis muttered. "You're a wanted man."

EIGHT

GREG AND ARAMIS EXITED THE HÔTEL DE VILLE TO FIND the Place de Grève crawling with soldiers.

Greg nearly froze in fear, but Aramis pulled him along. "Relax. They're not looking for you. There has been much civil unrest here, so the king has posted them to keep the peace. Just keep your head down and act natural and we'll get out of here."

Act natural? That's what had made him a marked man in the first place. Acting natural meant sticking out like Aramis would stick out in the twenty-first century.

"Who is Dominic Richelieu?" Greg did his best to mimic Aramis's accent as they slipped through the market stalls. He tried to remember his French history. "Is he the cardinal?"

"Cardinal?" Aramis laughed, despite himself. "Dominic Richelieu is no man of God. That's his brother, Armand... and *he's* only a bishop. Dominic is in charge of the king's guard."

"Would he listen to us?" Greg whispered hopefully.

Aramis sniffed. "I doubt it. Dominic is a despicable man. He manipulates the king and uses the guard as his own personal army. Your parents wouldn't be the first undeserving people he'd locked up in La Mort Triste. Anyone who crosses him is in grave danger."

"But if no one will listen to us, how do we get them out?"

Aramis didn't answer. He picked up his pace, his head down under his cowl.

"Stop that boy!" a voice shouted behind them.

Greg whirled around, panicked.

To his relief, the cry wasn't directed at him, but at a boy his age being chased through the plaza by a group of soldiers. The boy was dressed like a soldier, too, but he seemed... healthier. He was bigger; he wasn't as filthy as those pursuing him, and even though his blond hair was parted in the middle, it looked *combed*. Weirdest of all, he was smiling. And his teeth seemed fairly white. He reminded Greg of the captain of the Wellington Prep football team.

When it was clear he was cornered, the boy paused in the central courtyard—surrounded by at least twenty soldiers.

"This boy is to be arrested for mutinous behavior!" the voice cried again.

Greg flinched. His eyes zeroed in on Captain Valois, the mustached jerk who'd pursued him to Notre Dame the night before.

"All I did was prove that my commander had no business leading a brigade," the boy replied. Then he grinned at a few girls watching the drama, who giggled and blushed.

"By attacking your commander?" Valois shot back. He glared at the girls. "And there is nothing funny here!"

"If a commander can't defeat one of his own men in battle, then what qualifies him to lead?" the boy asked. He withdrew a gleaming silver sword from the sheath at his side.

Instead of answering, the soldiers lunged at him. The boy parried all their swords in a single sweeping stroke: *clack-clack-clack-clack*. Then he spun and slashed through a rope that bound several kegs of wine in a tall pyramid. The boy sprang away as the kegs rolled free, scattering his attackers. Greg found himself smiling as the boy scampered through the chaos, searching for an escape.

Aramis tugged at Greg's sleeve. "Let's leave while this fool diverts the militia."

Greg didn't budge. An idea came to him. The boy was the most incredible swordsman he'd ever seen, besting the soldiers without breaking a sweat. "We could use him," Greg murmured.

"Him? He's fighting an entire brigade! He's insane!"

"Exactly the type of person I need," Greg answered.

The boy battled as valiantly as he could: bashing one soldier in the nose with a thigh from a butcher's stall, clobbering another over the head with a fresh melon, jabbing an ox in the rear with his sword and startling it into stampeding toward three others. But he was greatly outnumbered. The remaining soldiers swarmed him next to a long table piled high with fish—stripping his sword from his grasp. One soldier held him tight. Within a second, Valois was there to point his own sword at the boy's throat.

"Take him to La Mort," the captain demanded with a sneer.

The boy suddenly whipped his head back into the nose of the soldier who held him. The soldier howled in pain and released the boy.

Valois attacked, but the boy snatched a swordfish off the table and defended himself with its spearlike nose— quickly disarming Valois. A cheer rose from the girls in the crowd. The boy somersaulted off the table and bent to snatch his own sword off the cobblestones.

As he did, another soldier lunged out of the crowd behind him, preparing to stab him in the back.

"Look out!" Greg yelled, before he could think better of it.

The boy spun and dodged the soldier's sword—but Valois swung his attention toward Greg.

"You!" he gasped, then called to his men. "Forget the mutineer! That's our assassin!"

Greg felt the color drain from his face. He and Aramis fled through the market toward the house-lined bridge that led back to Île de la Cité. Valois's men raced after them.

"Nicely done," Aramis chided Greg. "Now *you're* going to end up in La Mort as well."

Greg knew he was right. He cursed himself for being so foolish. He could hear the soldiers closing in from behind. . . .

The boy suddenly pulled up alongside him, close enough for Greg to see he had bright green eyes. "Keep going!" he ordered. "I'll take care of them." With that, he whirled around and upended a cart piled high with live eels. The fish spilled across the road. The soldiers slipped and skidded on the writhing mass of slippery bodies, going down like dominoes.

With their pursuers in disarray, the three boys raced across the bridge—not even pausing to look back. Greg's lungs burned, but he kept running until the three of them had slipped behind the safety of the walls of Notre Dame.

Greg turned to the boy with gratitude; he could have escaped once the soldiers had been distracted, but instead he'd returned to the fray to save Greg and Aramis.

"Thank you," Greg panted.

The boy shook his head. "No, it is I who owe *you* thanks. I wouldn't have needed to save you if you hadn't saved me first. I am forever indebted to you."

"I don't suppose you'd like to help us with a mission, then?" Greg asked.

Aramis glared at Greg, but was too out of breath to protest.

The boy's eyes lit up with excitement. "What sort of mission?"

Before Greg could answer, Aramis stepped between them. "This is a mistake," he said. "We shouldn't be consorting with a mutineer."

"I'm no mutineer," the boy responded. "All I did was challenge my superior officer to a swordfight."

"And why would you do such a thing?" Aramis asked scornfully.

"My officer was a fool who had his position only because his family purchased it for him. He had no business commanding a platoon. I was simply trying to prove that. My officer agreed to step down if I won. Which I did. But instead of stepping down, he accused me of mutiny."

"That makes two of us who've been falsely accused of something," Greg said, looking at Aramis. "And my parents have been unfairly imprisoned in La Mort Triste. We're looking for someone to help break them out."

The boy stared at Greg, then broke into laughter. "La Mort Triste! You're crazy!"

"See?" Aramis said to Greg. "Even *he* thinks it's impossible."

"Nothing is impossible," the boy inserted, still chuckling. "Some things are just incredibly difficult. Luckily for you, I love a good challenge. And now, apparently, I am unemployed and in your debt." The boy shook Greg's hand and said something that Greg wasn't *entirely* surprised to hear. "My name is Athos."

NINE

"THAT IS THE UGLIEST BUILDING I HAVE EVER SEEN," GREG announced.

"Of course it is," Aramis replied.

"Ugliness is fear," Athos added.

Greg decided not to ask what he meant. He realized now more than ever that it was best to focus on the positives— just as he'd been trying to do even before he'd been sucked through a giant painting back in time. And right now, things were looking up. For one, he had now befriended two of the Musketeers. For another, he was outside of the city. It was a beautiful afternoon. The three boys stood on the bank of the Seine a half mile east of Paris, in a pleasant countryside of rolling hills and serene fields. Upriver from the city, the water of the Seine was so clear Greg could see trout swimming along the bottom.

But La Mort Triste was a blight on the landscape: a dark, squat lump perched on an island in the middle of the river. To Greg, it looked like a giant cinder block with turrets.

"Any mason worth his salt is working on the Louvre," Aramis explained. "Or a cathedral or a château for some noble. No one wants to build a prison. Though as you can see, the designer did incorporate the latest in prison technology into the design."

"What's that?" Greg asked.

Aramis turned to him, surprised. "Why, the river, of course! Even if someone managed to break out of their cell and scale the walls, they'd drown."

"Unless they could swim," Greg countered.

Both boys burst out laughing.

"What?" Greg mumbled, embarrassed.

"Who can swim, other than characters from Roman myths?" Athos asked.

Greg shrugged. "I can."

Athos stared at Greg as though he'd said he could fly. "I've never met anyone who could swim. That's why they built the prison on that godforsaken island in the first place. That's why they put moats around castles! How on earth do you know how to swim?"

"Uh . . . everyone I know back home can do it."

Aramis shook his head. "Artagnan must be some amazing place. You can all swim. You have more planets than we do. Next thing I know, you'll tell me you can cook a meal in less than a day."

Greg decided not to reply to that. "That's really why they built the prison there?"

"*One* of the reasons," Aramis said. "It's also easier to get rid of all the dead bodies when you can just dump them in the river. And it keeps all the disease away from the city."

Greg swallowed hard. "What disease?"

"The plague, mostly," Aramis replied. "Leprosy, too. Just about everyone who goes in there gets sick. The Lord doesn't care for sinners."

"They're not getting sick because God is angry at them," Greg objected. "The conditions in the prison make them sick."

"That's what they say in Artagnan, is it?" Aramis asked.

Greg realized there was no point in arguing. It didn't matter what anyone believed about disease: Consignment to La Mort was a death sentence. Worse, Greg could see why the prison had a reputation for being impenetrable. There were no windows and only one door: a huge slab of oak—right in front of the lone dock, flanked by two guards. Then there were the guards on the roof, shuttling along parapets between the turrets at each corner. With so many men on patrol, there was no way to approach the prison without being seen.

"If I had my own brigade, I could get in there," Athos remarked wistfully.

Aramis sniffed. "Someone like you will never command a brigade."

Greg turned from the prison and frowned. "What did you just say?"

"This Athos is from a lower class," Aramis replied simply. "Not educated."

"So what?" Greg heard himself snap. "Why *shouldn't* Athos be able to lead a brigade? Shouldn't the best soldier be given that job? What about that clown we found at the Hôtel de Ville? Is it better to have someone who just *bought* the position?"

"Exactly my point!" Athos chimed in. "My commander was a clown."

"You don't know that," Aramis said to Greg, pointing at Athos. "You're only taking *his* word for it."

"My word has nothing to do with it," Athos argued. "The man's incompetence was a fact. He barely knew which end of a sword to hold."

"I'm sure he was better than that," Aramis said. "No nobleman could be that incompetent."

"Why?" Athos challenged. "Simply because he's a nobleman?"

"Yes," Aramis replied.

Athos snorted. "So then, you actually believe that all nobles are simply better than we are because they happened to be born above us?"

"I didn't create the world. The Lord did," Aramis stated.

"You didn't answer the question," Athos taunted.

Aramis glared at him hotly. "This is a dangerous line of thought. Once you start questioning the right of anyone to be above you, when does it stop? Do you believe the king himself is no better than any one of us?"

Athos paused. "Perhaps he isn't."

Aramis gasped in shock, and then turned to Greg. "We shouldn't be in league with this boy. He doesn't think properly."

Greg squinted in disbelief at the cleric. "You've honestly never asked yourself why the king gets to be king and not you?"

"Never," Aramis said.

"Not even for a second?" Greg prodded.

Aramis didn't answer right away. For a moment there appeared to be a flicker of doubt behind his eyes. But he took a deep breath and shook his head. "This is the way of the world. We are all born to our station in life. Can you imagine what would happen if we weren't? If we could all simply do whatever we wanted? It would be chaos."

"Not necessarily," Greg said earnestly.

"It would," Aramis said, as though it were a proven fact. "We all have our role to play. The king was born king. My brother was born first, not I. I can't change either of those things any more than a cow can try to become a person."

"I notice it's always the people on the top of the class system who say that," Athos mused. "Not the people on the bottom."

"I'm not on the top of the class system," Aramis protested.

"Well, you're higher up than me," Athos snapped.

Greg stood between them. "Enough! We'll never save my parents if we can't work as a team."

The boys glared at each other over Greg's shoulder, but remained silent.

"I fear this is a hopeless mission," Aramis said with a sigh, turning back to the prison. "It's protected by at least twenty men."

"I can defeat twenty men," Athos said with a smile. "I did it before lunch today."

"In a crowded marketplace," Aramis countered. "These soldiers have the advantage of high ground and open water. They could kill you a hundred times before you even got to the island."

"Then we'll just have to figure out a way for me to get to that island without being seen," Athos said.

"And what then?" Aramis asked. "How will you find Greg's parents? The prison is rumored to be a labyrinth inside."

Athos considered this, then said, "We'll have to talk to someone who has been inside La Mort."

"Ha!" Aramis barked. "Good luck with that. Anyone who goes inside La Mort either comes out to be hanged or comes out as a corpse."

"I wasn't thinking of a prisoner," said Athos.

"Fine, but its guards have all sworn not to reveal details of the prison's construction under penalty of death," Aramis stated.

Athos shrugged. "I wasn't thinking of a guard, either."

"Then who?" Greg asked.

Athos's green eyes danced. "Someone I haven't met but have heard of more than once. His name is Porthos. He's not only been inside La Mort, he's lived to tell the tale."

TEN

Aramis suggested that it might be best if he tracked down Porthos while Greg and Athos hid in his room in Notre Dame. Aramis was the only one who wasn't a wanted man, after all. But the real truth, Greg suspected, was that Aramis could tell Greg was exhausted. Not for the first time, Greg thought how lucky he was to have met Aramis, someone who looked out for others to such a degree. There was no doubt that Aramis lent him legitimacy and had probably contributed to Athos's decision to join the quest. Greg found himself looking up gratefully to both new friends, as if to a pair of wildly different older brothers.

Both Greg and Athos fell asleep on the straw pallet, Greg too bone-tired to think for long about the way the future Musketeers were all coming together.

The room was dark when Aramis shook Greg and Athos awake. "I've found Porthos," he whispered. "It wasn't hard."

Greg was too groggy to ask any questions. He shambled into a borrowed cloak and followed Aramis and Athos out into the Parisian night, across the house-lined bridge. Only this time, they headed away from the Hôtel de Ville, toward an area of town that was nicer than the ones Greg had seen before. Stone homes lined the streets. Horse-drawn carriages rattled over cobblestones, and Athos stole resentful glances at the passengers. All were decked out in finery, with silk robes and glittering jewels. Their perfume reeked. But at least it was better than the smell of body odor.

"Just one of those gems could feed my neighbors for a year," Athos muttered.

The farther they plodded along, the clearer it became that every carriage was headed to the same place: a massive château that loomed at a dead end. Athos pointed toward a wobbly figure standing in the shadows at one side.

Greg's eyes narrowed. The boy was . . . peeing.

"That's Porthos," Aramis whispered irritably.

The boy buttoned his pants, then turned and staggered

back into the moonlight. Two teenage girls appeared from seemingly out of nowhere and looped their arms around his. The boy cackled with laughter. Greg wasn't sure if he wanted to laugh himself. Porthos wore foppish clothes: a velvet jacket and a wide-brimmed hat with a feather. He was also slightly overweight, which made him the fattest person Greg had seen so far in 1615. Most people were borderline emaciated. So Porthos was clearly rich. No wonder he was carefree and happy and relieving himself where he wanted.

"He's a ne'er-do-well," Aramis spat.

"If there was ever an argument against the class system, he's it," Athos snorted.

"Come along, Porthos!" one of the girls cried, her bouffant hairdo swaying in the night breeze. "Let's get back to the party."

"The party *is* me," Porthos joked. "I am the party."

Both girls tittered in response.

Greg stepped forward and tapped Porthos on the shoulder. "Sorry to bother you," he said. "My friends and I would like to ask you some questions about a particular area of expertise you have."

Porthos considered him curiously. "I wasn't aware I *had* an area of expertise," he finally replied.

"We hear you've been inside La Mort," Athos chimed in.

Porthos's ruddy face brightened. "Ah! Yes, I have. Though if you're looking for a story, I have many that are better. I could start with the time the Lord of Buckingham challenged me to a duel. But I'm sure you've heard *that* one."

The girls giggled, as if on cue.

"It's La Mort that interests us," Aramis said. "It's a matter of life and death."

"Well. This sounds terribly serious." Porthos turned to the girls. "Don't worry, ladies. It's not a bad tale either. Come inside, everyone." He hooked an arm around each of the girls' waists and headed for the door.

Greg started after him, but Aramis seized his arm.

"We can't go in there!" Aramis hissed. "That's a nobleman's house!"

Porthos turned and laughed. "First of all, you're with me, so you can come. Second, it's a party. No one will even notice you." With that, he marched up the front steps and puffed out his chest toward the servants who flanked the open door: two anxious-looking older boys in red coats. Voices, laughter, and the faint strains of tinny classical music trickled outside—carried on the scent of a delicious roast. Greg's mouth watered.

"Lord Porthos of Tremblay returning with his entourage," Porthos announced.

The servants bowed graciously to him and allowed the entire group inside, though Greg caught them both frowning at him and Aramis and Athos. Greg kept his head down and hurried after Porthos and his two girlfriends.

For the first time since Greg had arrived in the past, he

found himself in a somewhat familiar setting. A party for rich kids in 1615 looked a lot like a party for rich kids four centuries later—only the music was softer (a mandolin trio accompanied by a harpsichord), the makeup was a lot thicker . . . and the fashion was so over the top that Greg had to bite his lip to keep from laughing.

"What's with the huge wigs?" Greg heard himself ask.

"Fleas. Lice." Aramis whispered back. "Maybe in Artagnan, they've found a way to rid the world of them. But here in Paris, shaving one's head is a sign of nobility."

Some guests wore wigs so tall that the owners had to duck under the candlelit chandeliers. On the dance floor, couples simply moved in prearranged patterns. It looked like an old-time American square dance, but slower and a lot less fun.

"This is unbelievable," Athos muttered, shaking his head in disgust.

"It is," Aramis answered serenely. "I've never seen so much food in my life."

Greg followed their eyes. Three roast pigs sat in the center of a massive wooden table near the musicians— surrounded by a cornucopia of fruits, vegetables, soups, sauces, cheeses, charcuterie, nuts, spices, and platters of flaky pastries. Without thinking, Greg ravenously descended on the feast, followed by Athos and Aramis. He tried to ignore the fact that several guests were frowning at them as they stuffed their faces.

Luckily, Porthos swept in and began shoving roast pig into his mouth along with them. He also tucked a few extra pastries into the folds of his shirt. Greg reached for a tiny silver bowl.

"What are you doing?" Porthos asked curiously.

"Just getting some cinnamon."

"It costs more per ounce than gold," Porthos whispered.

Greg swallowed. Now that his hunger had been partially sated, he realized that there were only two other silver bowls on the table, each atop a small pedestal. One held salt and one held pepper. "Sorry. Cinnamon isn't valuable where I come from."

Porthos's bushy eyebrows wrinkled. "Where is that? The East Indies?"

"He's from Artagnan, my lord," Aramis explained.

"Ahh." Porthos smiled again. "That explains the strange accent, too. So why are you so interested in La Mort?" he asked, his mouth crammed full.

"My parents have been sent there," Greg answered.

"Bad news for them. What'd they do?"

"Nothing," Greg said anxiously. "They were accused unjustly."

"Just like me!" Porthos exclaimed.

Athos laughed. "I heard you stole a horse from the Lord of Bordeaux."

"Pfft." Porthos sniffed. "His son lost that horse in a card game to me but didn't want to admit it to his father. He said it was stolen, and I got nabbed for riding it."

"And they put *you* in La Mort?" Aramis asked.

Porthos wiped his mouth with his velvet coat sleeve. "I didn't look noble when they caught me."

"What do you mean?" Greg asked, confused.

"I fell off the horse," Porthos admitted. "Into the Seine." He laughed. "I'm not the best rider. And it was a very spirited horse. I got soaked and it was a cold day, so I procured clothes from some peasants. When the militia caught up to me, I *looked* like a peasant. I had no way to prove my name, so they tossed me into La Mort. Fortunately, when Bordeaux's son heard what had happened, he notified my parents. They notified Dominic Richelieu of the mistake. He released me."

"How long were you inside?" Greg asked.

"A day." Porthos turned away with a shudder and grabbed a handful of dried fruit. "Worst day of my life . . ."

Athos leaned forward. "Could you describe what the inside of the prison was like?"

Porthos smirked. "You're *sure* you wouldn't rather hear about my duel with Buckingham?"

Greg suppressed a smile. He found himself liking Porthos more and more by the minute. "Later. For now, we want to hear about the prison."

Porthos sighed, disappointed.

"If you can, tell us everything you can remember," Aramis said. "How it's laid out. How the door works. The number of guards posted inside—"

Porthos's smile faded. He shot a wary glance among the three of them. "Why do you want this information? You all almost sound like you're planning a prison break. . . ."

Greg jerked involuntarily. They had been too obvious. His face reddened.

But Porthos's eyes went wide with excitement. So far, it seemed he'd been indulging them as a diversion, keeping one eye on the party in case someone more interesting came along. But now, for the first time, he stared at Greg with a peculiar intensity. "You are, aren't you? And people say *I'm* crazy!"

Greg met his gaze. "These are my parents. And like you, they were unjustly accused. We have no other option."

"With only two clerics and one soldier?" Porthos laughed. "You can't possibly expect to succeed."

"I'm a very good soldier," Athos stated.

"And he's very smart," Greg said, pointing to Aramis.

"And what do *you* bring to the party, D'Artagnan?" Porthos demanded of Greg.

Greg withered under his gaze, finally admitting, "Not much. But they're my parents. I can't just let them die."

"Of course not." Porthos suddenly grew solemn. "I had a cellmate in La Mort. He claimed he was innocent, that Richelieu had falsely accused him of a crime. I thought this man was a liar. Everyone in prison says they're innocent, right? But then, a few months later, I met the man's brother at a dice game. The brother confirmed the truth: This man had been imprisoned on Richelieu's whim—and died inside La Mort." Porthos frowned. For the first time, his jolly demeanor faded. "I've never done anything important—anything that really mattered, I mean. No one's ever asked me to. And now you're being too shy to ask. But if your parents are truly innocent . . . I would like to help you."

"You would?" Greg asked, excited. "You mean—"

"Stop!" Aramis interrupted. "Porthos. You want to *join* us? Didn't you just say we couldn't expect to succeed?"

"*Three* people couldn't," Porthos countered. "But with my help . . ."

"Help?" Athos spat. "Everyone in Paris knows who you are! Just tell us about La Mort. That's all the help we need from you."

Porthos straightened, clumsily attempting to unsheathe his sword. "Perhaps you'd like to step outside and see how good a swordsman I am."

Athos simply stepped forward and shoved Porthos down on an ornate sofa. A hushed murmur rose from the crowd, and the music seemed to skip a beat, but Porthos waved to everyone with a grin. In an instant, everything returned to normal.

"All right, I'm not the best swordsman," he said. "But I do have other skills. Like getting people to do what I want. Or what *we* want." He looked at Greg.

Athos and Aramis both turned to Greg as well.

Greg shrugged. "Porthos is right. This is going to be hard enough with only three people. We can use all the help we can get." He returned his attention to Porthos. "If we get you into La Mort, could you find my parents and help get them out?"

"I very much doubt it," Porthos admitted. "But—"

"Then what good are you?" Athos demanded.

"You didn't let me finish!" Porthos snapped. "I was trying to say, 'But we need a map.' La Mort is a maze that is dark as the stormiest night."

"So where do they keep the map?" Aramis asked. "Inside the guards' quarters?"

"Oh no," Porthos replied. "Then anyone who broke in would be able to use it."

"Then how do the guards find their way around?" Athos inquired.

"They have to memorize the place," Porthos said. "And good luck getting any of them to tell you anything. The penalty for that is death."

"So . . . there *isn't* any map?" Greg asked.

"No, there *is*. But it's not at La Mort," Porthos said. "From what I understand, Dominic Richelieu keeps a copy in his office."

"Inside the Louvre?" Aramis replied, looking queasy.

Porthos nodded and turned to Greg. "If you want to rescue your parents, we're going to need it."

Greg slumped beside Porthos on the couch, feeling exhausted again. "So you're saying that we now also have to break into the king's palace?"

Porthos threw a friendly arm around Greg's shoulder. "Don't worry. I don't only know my way around La Mort. I *also* know my way around the Louvre."

ELEVEN

Porthos invited Greg, Athos, and Aramis to spend the night in his own family's city home: a smaller château in the same neighborhood. Greg was thrilled. Anything besides straw was an improvement, and in Porthos's house he was shown by servants to a soft mattress stuffed with feathers. He fell asleep in an instant.

Porthos himself shook Greg awake, shoving an apple into his face. "Eat this. We've got planning to do."

Greg sat up and rubbed his eyes, squinting around the

room. Aramis and Athos were already up and alert. The sun glared through the window. Greg took a bite of the apple and mustered his thoughts.

"Look," he began, "I have no money to repay you . . . and I know this quest has only a slim chance of succeeding. I guess I just wanted to say . . . thank you. I don't know why the three of you would go to such lengths to help me, a stranger. But I am truly—"

"By now you're not a stranger," Aramis interrupted. "You're a friend."

"Besides, this is about right and wrong, and defending honor," Athos added.

"And it's so much more interesting than anything else I've got going on," Porthos concluded with a wink.

Greg found himself grinning. The dread that had been sitting heavy in his heart seemed to lighten, even if only slightly. "Then let's do this!" he said.

"Porthos has a plan," Aramis said, turning to the chubby boy.

"I've been invited to plenty of parties at the palace, so I can find my way around inside," Porthos began. "Once we get in, we'll work our way over to Richelieu's office, which is in the military wing. I assume you've been there . . . ?" He looked to Athos.

"Only once," Athos said. "I had to register there when I joined the militia."

"Ah, yes. The militia." Porthos smiled. "That's where

you come in, Athos—"

"Wait," Greg interjected. "How do we get into the palace in the first place?"

"Through the front door." Porthos stared at him as if he were an idiot. "How else would you enter a palace?"

"But how?" Greg asked. "Isn't the door guarded?"

"Of course. There are two soldiers posted there," Porthos said.

"And we're just supposed to walk right past them?" Greg asked.

"Certainly not," Porthos replied. "They *lead* us in."

Greg opened his mouth but decided not to argue. After all, he and Aramis had marched right into the Hôtel de Ville without any advance warning, and they'd gotten every piece of information they'd needed. Security was a joke in 1615. It wasn't as if there were ID cards or retinal scans or fingerprints . . . or even signatures. People relied on words and appearance—period.

Porthos went on to explain that official delegations from all over the civilized world often arrived at the palace, but the guards rarely ever knew who was coming until they got there. In fact, more delegations than usual had been arriving recently as His Majesty King Louis XIII was preparing to marry Princess Anne of Austria. The best any visitor could provide was an official letter from whoever had sent them, marked with an official wax seal.

Greg got it. If you wanted to access the palace, you only

needed to look the part and to carry an official-looking piece of paper. Porthos could provide it all.

Greg had been in such a hurry to escape the Louvre the last time he'd been there, he hadn't really looked at the outside of it. Now, as he approached it with the other three boys on Porthos's horses, what he saw astonished him.

The building was in the process of being converted from fortress to palace, with three stories of scaffolding running along the entire length. Stonemasons swarmed over it like ants; there seemed to be hundreds. The sound of all their hammers banging away at stone could be heard from half a mile away.

The main entrance to the palace was almost lost in the scaffolding. It was surprisingly unimpressive: a set of weathered wooden doors with a few crumbling stone steps leading up to them. The entrance to Porthos's home was nicer. Two soldiers were posted near it, but neither was as attentive as Greg had expected. Both sat in the shade of the scaffolding, obviously bored. One polished his sword on his sleeve; the other appeared to be daydreaming. They didn't appear much older than Greg.

And yet, they were still soldiers. Greg grew nervous as they came closer—and noticed Aramis did, too.

"This is never going to work," the cleric said. "We'll end up in La Mort all right, as prisoners ourselves."

"Ye of little faith," Porthos said with his usual cocky

93

smile. "The more confident we appear, the less they'll question us. Everything will be fine. Trust me."

"Easy for you to say," Athos grumbled. The plan required him to wear his usual militia uniform *under* the fine silks Porthos had lent him. He was dripping with sweat.

Greg, on the other hand, had never felt better in nobleman's clothing. For the first time since he'd arrived in the past, he didn't itch all over. Both he and Aramis were fully costumed in clothes raided from Porthos's wardrobe. Porthos had even tucked a tiny sapphire in Greg's linen glove "For when the time comes to bargain."

"Porthos, wait," Aramis cautioned. "If you've been here for parties, won't they recognize you?"

"Do *you* know everyone who comes to Mass on Sundays at Notre Dame?" Porthos asked.

Aramis shook his head.

"Exactly," Portos said. "*Lots* of people come to these parties. Every nobleman for miles around. No one knows who's who. And besides, it's been a few months since I've been here. I've grown a few inches since then."

"Yeah, around your waist," Athos muttered.

The soldiers at the main entrance snapped to attention when they saw the four horsemen nearing. Greg's pulse picked up a notch.

"Who approaches the home of His Majesty King Louis XIII?" the first soldier called.

The four boys dismounted their horses, holding their

heads high as if they were all nobility. Porthos marched up the steps and handed the soldier a false letter of introduction Aramis had written. "I am Lord Vincennes from Bordeaux, here to pay my respect to the king."

The soldiers snapped the wax seal open and glanced at the paper.

Greg's heart squeezed. The letter was upside down. But neither soldier noticed. Apparently, both were illiterate. They seemed impressed by the look of it, however.

"The king has done us great service in Bordeaux," Porthos said. "My family wishes to offer our thanks with this gift." He waved dramatically to Greg, who took the cue. He removed his glove and produced the sapphire.

The soldiers gaped at it with awe and then nodded approval. The second guard remained to mind the horses while the first ushered the four boys inside. Greg kept the sapphire clutched tightly in his fist.

"Is the king expecting you?" the guard asked as the boys followed him through the main hall.

"No," Porthos replied. "I had other business in Paris and decided to drop by."

"You probably won't be able to see him, then," the guard said. "The king is a very busy man. But one of his secretaries might be available to meet with you in his stead."

Porthos nodded distantly. "That would be fine."

Greg's chest thumped as they marched up the wooden staircase he'd fled down two nights before. He tried not to glance up at the chandelier. At the landing, they turned in a different direction. In the rooms that lined this long hall, first attempts were under way at making the Louvre the beautiful building it would ultimately become. Craftsmen and painters were hard at work on a large salon; carpenters were laying down a new wood floor and sculpting decorations for the walls; glaziers were installing new windows. And painters were filling the ceiling with white clouds and cherubs.

The soldier paused in front of a massive double door and waved the foursome to a pair of upholstered benches. "Wait here, if you please. I'll alert the king's staff as to your presence."

Porthos cleared his throat. "Before you go, my men and I have ridden a long way today and drunk much water. Is there a place for us to go . . . relieve ourselves?"

"There is a privy for guests to the right of the main stairs," the soldier replied.

"Ah. I think we can find that," Porthos said.

"Very well, sir." The soldier exited with their letter of introduction, leaving them alone and unguarded.

The moment he was gone, the boys slipped back out the way they'd come.

"That ought to buy us at least a quarter hour," Porthos said with a snicker.

Greg had to laugh, too. Porthos might have been the first person in history to ever think of the ruse of asking for the bathroom in order to escape. Porthos led the way back down the grand staircase, then through a long stretch of palace that was still unfinished—muddy and roughhewn. From the smell, it seemed they were close to the stables. Greg guessed he had run above this area two nights before.

They eventually passed another wide but rickety staircase and arrived in an empty hall. Athos signaled everyone to be on guard. Porthos nodded.

"What's going on?" Greg asked.

"This is where the militia is headquartered," Athos replied. He pointed toward the lone door at the end of the corridor. "Richelieu's office is right over there."

The door to Richelieu's office wasn't locked—there *was* no lock—and it was deserted. The office was large, with a wooden desk, a high-backed chair, and a long row of cabinets along the wall behind it. A framed map of Paris hung on the right wall, facing a framed map of France on the left. Unlike the office door, however, every drawer and cabinet was locked.

"This is going to take some time," Greg said, sighing. "Looks like we'll need a sentry."

Athos nodded. He peeled off Porthos's clothes, revealing his uniform. True, he'd been kicked out of the militia. But only his superior officer and the men in his unit knew what he looked like. To anyone else, he would simply appear to be a regular soldier. He slipped outside and posted himself in the hall, closing the door behind him.

Aramis studied the labels on the cabinets, written in a language neither Greg nor Porthos could understand. But Greg thought it looked like—

"Latin," Aramis stated. "This top drawer holds information related to La Mort."

"Stand back." Porthos whipped out his sword and approached the credenza.

"What are you doing?" Greg asked, panicked.

Porthos didn't answer. He jammed his sword through the narrow slit near the lock and placed his considerable weight on it. The wood splintered and the lock broke.

Aramis glared at Porthos. "You have no respect for others' property?"

"Not when peoples' lives hang in the balance," Porthos muttered.

Greg opened the cabinet and began rifling through the stacks of parchment. The other boys helped, though it still took several minutes to go through it all. There was no map, only lists of those incarcerated . . . and, ominously, execution orders. Greg's heart began to pound again. They had squandered precious time.

"It's not here," Aramis said, disheartened. "Let's get out while we can." He started for the door.

Greg stayed rooted to the spot, however, his mind racing. Why wasn't the map of La Mort in the drawer? Did it even exist? Had it been removed for some reason? Or were they just looking in the wrong place . . . ?

A thought suddenly came to him. "We're looking for an architectural plan. Is there a cabinet for those?"

Aramis pointed at another drawer. "There!"

Porthos quickly thrust his sword into the narrow crack at the top of the drawer—and with a mighty grunt, snapped both the lock and his sword into pieces. He cursed under his breath. Greg, on the other hand, felt a surge of hope. Piled in the drawer were stacks of floor plans—exactly what they needed.

Greg and the others dug through them quickly, wantonly flinging the rejections aside. It seemed as though every building in Paris was represented.

There was an urgent knock at the door.

"We need to leave!" Athos hissed from the other side. "An entire squad is coming!"

Aramis and Porthos grabbed stacks of parchment, but Greg stayed put. He was almost through his pile, his fingers flying through the pages . . .

There! At the very bottom of his pile, Greg found a page filled with a jumble of passageways and the heading "*Le Labyrinthe de La Mort Triste.*"

"I've got it!" he yelled, holding it up triumphantly.

Athos threw the door open. "Move. Now!" he shouted.

Greg, Athos, and Porthos fled from the room to find a dozen soldiers coming down the hall toward them. Greg scrambled after the other boys, heading back toward the front door. As they passed the staircase, they spotted a second group of guards coming, cutting off their escape route.

"Upstairs!" Porthos shouted, leading the way.

As Greg followed, he noticed another massive, candle-laden chandelier hanging above—like the one he'd swung from on the other side of the Louvre.

"Athos!" he shouted, pointing to the support rope. "Cut that!"

Athos hurled his sword, slicing straight through it. The chandelier plummeted in a blaze of flame and smoke. The soldiers scattered as it smashed to the floor, blocking the stairs.

All three boys turned to Greg at the top of the stairwell, impressed.

"How'd you ever come up with that?" Aramis gasped.

"Where I come from . . . it's kind of a cliché," Greg admitted.

Below, the soldiers began to clamber over the smashed chandelier.

"C'mon," Porthos said. He led the boys through a series of zigzagging passageways until he came to a small alcove. There he pressed a panel in the wall, and a hidden door slid open.

"How did you know about . . . ?" Aramis began.

"Like I said, I've been to parties here," Porthos replied proudly. Then, hearing the sounds of soldiers charging through the halls, he hustled the boys inside and slammed the door behind them.

There was a chorus of high-pitched gasps.

The boys spun around to find a dozen teenage girls staring at them. Greg's face grew hot. Aramis bowed his head.

Athos broke into a huge smile. "Now *this* is what I call a hiding place," he said.

TWELVE

Greg wasn't as taken with the girls as Athos and Porthos. They all had matted hair and wore dull, shapeless frocks that looked a lot like burlap sacks. Probably servants. Instead, his eyes glazed over at the opulence of the huge bedroom: overstuffed couches and ottomans covered with silk pillows, a vanity with three huge mirrors, and an enormous canopy bed. The walls were painted with fairies and woodland scenes, and ornate vases overflowed with fresh flowers.

"We shouldn't be in here," Aramis whispered.

"On the contrary," Athos said. "This is the *perfect* place for us to be." He stepped forward and flashed a sly smile. "Good afternoon, my ladies. It's a pleasure to meet you—" He broke off in midsentence, his jaw hanging open.

Another girl had entered from the far side of the room, decked out in a blue satin gown covered with lace and embroidered roses. But even if she had worn only a burlap frock, she would have captured everyone's attention. Her skin was porcelain and spotless, her blond hair done up in an elaborate bun. But most striking of all were her riveting blue eyes. Greg guessed she was about sixteen. "How dare you enter the queen's chambers!" she barked.

Porthos chuckled, the only one of the four boys who was unfazed. "I wasn't aware we had a queen," he replied.

"Then you are more foolish than you look. The whole world knows that Anne of Austria is betrothed to Louis. These will be her private chambers once they are wed, and no man is to step foot in them. Not even His Majesty King Louis himself! Now leave at once—or I shall call upon our soldiers to remove you by force."

Uh-oh. As she spoke, Greg heard approaching footsteps in the hall outside. Before either Porthos or Athos could utter another word, Greg leaped forward.

"We are terribly sorry to intrude, madamoiselle," he apologized. "But we are here at risk to our own lives to deliver a message of great importance to the queen."

The girl shifted her cold gaze to Greg. "I am to be the

queen's handmaiden. Any message delivered to me will get to her. What is it?"

Greg's mind whirled, making up the excuse as he went along. "There is a plot against her. Unfortunately, there are many in the king's own guard who may be involved. They cannot know we are here. You must trust us."

At that moment, the soldiers pounded on the true door to the room. "Open up in there!" a familiar voice demanded. "This is the king's guard."

That voice! It belonged to Valois. Greg's blood ran cold.

The girl studied the boys carefully, her gaze flickering as she paused on Aramis. His face was still beet red. His eyes remained pinned to the floor. A smile curled on the girl's lips. For the briefest moment, it seemed her pale face had softened. But just as quickly, she whirled and snapped her fingers at them. "Step behind the drapes," she hissed.

The boys quickly obeyed, ducking behind a suffocating wall of thick velvet. Once they were hidden from sight, the girl opened the door to face Valois and his men. Greg held his breath.

"What brings this intrusion to the queen's quarters?" she demanded.

"We apologize for the imposition, *mademoiselle*," Valois answered in a formal tone. "We seek some boys who have infiltrated the palace. They have stolen some valuable documents, and we believe they may have come this way."

"Well, I have not seen any boys," the girl answered.

"None of us have. And we have been here all morning."

"If you could allow us to quickly search . . ." Valois started over the threshold, but the girl held her ground.

"The king himself has not set foot in this room," she stated. "Do you think he would appreciate the news that *you* have?"

There was a long moment of silence. Greg exchanged a silent glance with the other boys. Nobody moved. Porthos was smiling, however, as if having a blast.

Valois cleared his throat. "This is a matter of great importance—"

"As is the sanctity of these chambers," the girl interrupted. "I can assure you the boys you seek are not here."

"Then I ask for your pardon, *mademoiselle*," Valois grumbled. There was a scuffle of footsteps as he retreated into the hall, and the door slammed behind him. Greg heaved a huge sigh of relief. For the second time, Valois had been headed off at the gate.

The girl stormed back across the room and flung the drapes aside. "You have exactly one minute to explain to me this plot against the queen. If I don't like what I hear, I'll call back the royal guard and you'll be sent to the gallows before sunset."

"It, um, it's actually quite simple," Greg began.

"I'm not asking you. I'm asking *him*." The girl pointed to Aramis. She flashed a wicked smile. "I have a feeling he's the most honest of you."

Porthos winced. "Now we're in trouble," he muttered.

Aramis stared into the girl's blue eyes. "Uh, well—you see—the truth is—there *is* no plot against the queen," he admitted.

Porthos, Athos, and Greg all groaned at the same time.

"*Ah!* I suspected as much." The girl frowned and strode for the door.

"Wait, we beg of you!" Aramis pleaded. "We are sorry to trespass. But the lives of two innocent people are at stake."

The girl stopped. Her eyes narrowed. Once again, she studied Aramis, as though trying to determine if she could trust him. "Then you had better explain yourself."

Aramis pointed to Greg. "This is D'Artagnan. Two nights ago, his parents were unfairly condemned to death by a man in the palace named Michel Dinicoeur."

"I have never heard of any man here with that name," the girl said.

"Neither has anyone else," Greg cut in. "However, I can assure you he exists. I've met him. And because of him, my parents are scheduled for execution the day after tomorrow. We are on a mission to save them."

"By breaking into the palace?" the girl asked. "How does that help anyone?"

"Well," Greg said, swallowing. "We, um, needed, to—"

"To petition His Majesty King Louis," Aramis finished. "He's the only one who can stop an execution."

The girl shifted her gaze. "So you came to see him

yourselves, is that right?"

"Desperate times call for desperate measures," Porthos replied cheerily.

Greg elbowed him in the side, but fortunately, Athos spoke up. "We felt it was worth the risk to our lives to save those of two innocent people." He smiled dramatically at the other girls in the room. Several smiled back.

The queen's handmaiden arched a perfectly trimmed eyebrow. "I see. What you have all done is either very brave . . . or very stupid."

"We were hoping for brave," Greg admitted. Suddenly a thought occurred to him. "*Mademoiselle*, I don't suppose that you—as the future queen's handmaiden—would have access to the king?"

The girl burst out laughing. "You're asking me to help you sneak into the quarters of His Majesty King Louis, knowing that if I get caught, I might be killed as well?"

"Er . . ." Greg blinked and shrugged, trying to smile. He couldn't quite muster the same charm as Porthos and Athos, though—and he knew it.

"Your bravado is incredible," the girl said.

"Thank you," Greg replied.

"That wasn't a compliment," said the girl with a sneer.

"Oh." Greg's ears burned.

"I've already taken a tremendous risk by not turning you over to those soldiers," she continued. "Why should I do any more?"

"Because if you don't help us, we'll have to force your hand," Athos said, whipping out his sword.

The queen's handmaiden suddenly spun in a blur of motion. A knife flew out of the folds of her gown and shot across the room—pinning Athos's sleeve to the wall less than an inch below his wrist. His sword clattered to the floor. Greg gasped in astonishment.

Athos simply chuckled. "What type of handmaiden is trained to use a blade like that?"

"One charged with protecting the queen's life." The girl hiked her skirt and produced another knife from her stocking. "Try a silly stunt again and the next one slits your throat."

Aramis stepped forward and raised both hands, positioning himself between the girl and Athos. "*Mademoiselle*, I apologize for Athos's rash behavior. All of us have risked our lives for this mission. We haven't had much rest, and our actions sometimes speak before our thoughts. You asked why you should help us. The only answer I can give is that it is the right thing to do. And the only reward we can offer is the pride in a good deed, and our eternal gratitude."

The girl stared at him for a long time. Finally she spoke to Athos. "Now *that* is how to negotiate with a woman. You would do well to learn from your friend."

"So . . . you'll take us to the king?" Greg asked, unable to contain his excitement.

"I'll *try*," said the girl. "I can't promise anything."

"Might I ask your name, *mademoiselle?*" Aramis inquired in a quiet voice.

"Milady. Milady de Winter."

"Thank you for your help, Milady de Winter." Aramis bowed respectfully.

She smiled again. "And might I ask your name, *monsieur?*"

"Aramis."

"It is my pleasure, Aramis."

"And I am Athos, at your service!" Athos cried, wrenching the knife from his sleeve.

"And I am Lord Porthos of Tremblay!" Porthos winked at some of the girls.

Greg stepped forward. "And I am—"

"D'Artagnan, yes, I know," Milady muttered impatiently, her attention still glued to Aramis. "We'll need to move fast. Stay right behind me and keep quiet. If you do as I say, maybe we'll all stay alive." She tucked the second knife back into her stocking and beckoned the foursome through the door by which she'd first entered.

Greg soon found himself scurrying to keep up. Milady whisked them through a labyrinth of narrow, torch-lit corridors. They barreled past an astonishing number of servants along the way—chefs, attendants, gardeners, stablemen, seamstresses, charwomen—all of whom gaped in surprise. Greg wondered if any of them would dash off to inform Valois and his men that there were strangers in the palace. But at least they all seemed as intimidated by Milady as he was.

Athos allowed Milady and Aramis to get a few paces ahead. "I'm not sure we should trust this girl," he whispered. "There's something about her I don't like."

"Would it be the fact that she likes Aramis and not *you*?" Porthos asked, amused.

Athos flushed but said nothing and continued on. Greg hurried after him, his pulse racing. Porthos seemed to think this was all a game, but what if Athos was right? What if Milady was leading them into a trap? Why *should* they trust her? She'd lied very convincingly to Valois, after all.

Ahead of them, at the intersection of two halls, Milady froze, listening intently to distant voices. "The guards . . . they're coming this way!" she gasped. She whirled and pointed at the vaulted door behind Greg. "Hide in there! I'll distract them. Quickly!"

Greg didn't hesitate. He yanked the door open, the other three boys piling in behind him. Porthos slammed the door. Greg squinted, blinded by a sudden glare of afternoon sunlight.

"Might I ask what you're doing here?" a boy's reedy voice demanded.

The silhouette of a frail figure stood before a massive window. As Greg's vision adjusted, he noticed that the boy's features were strange: his brown eyes were set oddly close together, and his nose was so pointy that it reminded Greg of a beak. In a city full of people in desperate need of a dentist, he had the worst teeth Greg had seen so far. To top it off, the boy wore a ridiculously frilly shirt and tight velvet leggings . . . and if he hadn't opened his mouth, his cascading hair would have pegged him for a girl.

"This is . . . um, Lord Vincennes of Bordeaux," Greg mumbled, pointing to Porthos. "We have some business with His Majesty King Louis. If you could—"

"You are incredibly ignorant," the boy snapped.

For a moment, Greg was annoyed. But coughs from the other boys caught his attention. To his surprise, they were all down on one knee, their heads bowed.

"I'd shut my mouth if I were you," Porthos warned under his breath. "That *is* His Majesty King Louis XIII."

THIRTEEN

ONCE AGAIN, GREG FOUND HIMSELF FROZEN STIFF. FORTU-
nately, a violent tug on his shirt snapped the spell, and he
dropped to a knee beside the others and bowed his head.
"That's the *king*?!" he whispered. "How old is he?"

"Your age. Fourteen," Aramis whispered back.

"He's been king since he was nine, you fool," Athos
hissed. "Does the news not reach Artagnan?"

"Don't answer that," Porthos told Greg. "And don't make
a move until you're spoken to, or you'll get us all killed."

In spite of the warning, Greg couldn't help but steal a

quick peek at the boy king, who stared back at them in unnerving silence. Greg bowed his head again. The room was surprisingly formal for a teenage boy, but then, Louis XIII was surprisingly formal himself. The furniture was all extremely ornate: wooden cabinets with elaborate inlaid designs, gilded mirrors, couches and lounges that were beautiful to look at but appeared uncomfortable to sit on. Thick draperies framed massive windows that should have looked out onto the palace courtyard—but now revealed only scaffolding. Giant portraits of Louis's ancestors hung on the walls—Greg thought he noticed one or two that were still in the modern Louvre—each in a wooden frame big enough to build a rowboat out of.

Greg kept expecting Milady to arrive and sort everything out with the king, and it seemed to him that the other boys did, too. But as the seconds ticked by, Porthos finally couldn't stand the silence any longer. He lifted his head and addressed the king. "Your Majesty, I would like to apologize for my friend's ignorance. He has only recently arrived in Paris from Artagnan."

"Ah. That explains your strange accent." Louis clasped his delicate hands together. Greg noticed that his nails were bright and shiny, in stark contrast to his teeth. "I've never been to that part of my empire. What's it like?"

Greg swallowed. He didn't know a thing about Artagnan, other than what he'd gleaned from Aramis. Instant wireless access to Wikipedia was four centuries away. "It's quite beautiful," he choked out.

"Ah, yes. So I've heard." Louis sounded pleased. "What is your name, boy?"

"My friends call me D'Artagnan."

"As a nickname, I suppose. But what is your family name?"

"Pamplemousse." It was the first French word that popped into Greg's head. But he immediately regretted his choice. *Pamplemousse* meant "grapefruit."

Porthos snickered beside him.

Louis knitted his brow. "That's an odd name. I thought I knew all the names of my nobles."

"Well, Your Highness," Porthos interrupted before Greg could dig himself into a deeper hole. "Artagnan is a far-flung region on the very edge of your empire. It is closer to Madrid than Paris."

"That's true," Louis concurred. "I can't be expected to know everyone. What is your business here, Pample-mousse?"

Porthos suppressed a laugh.

"I have come to petition for your help," Greg replied.

Louis looked perturbed. "My help? For what?"

"My parents have been falsely accused of treason and are sentenced to be hung two days from now."

Louis blinked and tapped his foot. He straightened his back, as if trying to act more kingly. But his eyebrows were tightly knit. It occurred to Greg that up until this point, Louis had merely been attempting to portray an image of royalty, because that was what was expected of him. But now, suddenly confronted with a life-or-death issue, the teenager in him showed through.

"Two people were captured in this palace two nights ago," he said finally. "I was told they were here to assassinate me."

"They weren't, Your Majesty," Greg replied sincerely.

Louis crossed the room slowly. "I was also told there was a boy with them who got away. I assume that was you?"

Greg considered lying but couldn't figure out how to spin the story fast enough. "Yes. But I promise you, my parents and I were framed. And now my parents are locked in La Mort Triste. We never had any intention to—"

"Then what *were* your intentions?" Louis demanded.

"A man stole something that belonged to my family," Greg explained. He swallowed hard. "A piece of jewelry. We followed him here to get it—"

"You came all the way from Artagnan just to pursue a thief?" Louis interrupted. "And then infiltrated my palace as well?"

"Uh . . . yes," Greg admitted.

"I do not consort with thieves," Louis snapped, sounding insulted. "What is the name of this man?"

"Michel Dinicoeur," Greg replied.

"There is no one here by that name," said the king.

Finally Porthos raised his head. "Is it possible you just don't know of him, Your Highness? Hundreds of people serve Your Majesty at the palace."

Louis thought for a moment, and then nodded. "Perhaps you're right. Let's get to the bottom of this, shall we?" He reached into his pocket and jingled a small brass bell.

A gray-haired servant who was old enough to be a grandfather immediately emerged from a side door. "Yes, Your Majesty . . . ?" He trailed off in surprise upon seeing the boys.

Louis beckoned him closer and whispered in his ear. The servant nodded obediently and hurried back out of the room. Louis flopped down on one of the couches, leaving them all kneeling on the floor. "That explains why you first broke into my palace. Why have you returned?"

"To appeal to you, Your Highness," Greg answered, hoping he sounded subservient enough.

"Why come to me?" Louis asked. "Why not go to those in charge of La Mort?"

Greg shook his head. "We tried. We met with a boy named Jacques Boule. But he said that you—Your Majesty—were the only person he would listen to."

"Really?" Louis seemed to be at a loss. "I don't know enough about the situation to render any judgment."

"With all due respect, Your Highness, you seem to have judged D'Artagnan's character already," Aramis pointed out. "If you felt threatened by him, you would have called for your soldiers, not a servant."

The king sniffed. It seemed this hadn't even occurred to

him. "You're right, I suppose. None of you appear dangerous, that's for certain."

"We don't mean you any harm, Your Majesty," Aramis stated. "We only seek your help, if you would bestow your grace upon us."

"Yes, yes. But I don't believe *his* story—not entirely." Louis swung his gaze back to Greg. "I've never heard of his family, never heard of this Michel Dinicoeur. . . ."

"I can vouch for D'Artagnan's honesty," Porthos said.

For the first time, the king smiled. "But can anyone vouch for yours, Porthos?" he asked, chuckling.

Porthos's jaw dropped.

"Yes, I know who you are," Louis said, waving his delicate hands dismissively. "You've been to a few parties here."

"But," Porthos began. "But there are always so many revelers—"

"And yet so very few who make such a scene," the king said. "You destroyed a family portrait last time you were here."

Porthos tried to match the king's smile. "That was an accident—"

"My cousin says you stole his horse," Louis countered.

"I won that from him fair and square!" Porthos shouted. He quickly bowed his head, his face reddening.

Louis laughed again. "You have quite a reputation for caring about nothing but having a good time."

"I care about many things," Porthos said defensively. He

peeked up at the king again. "But nobility is entitled to some fun, yes?"

"I'm not," Louis answered softly. He sagged in his seat.

The boys exchanged a quick, puzzled glance.

"You're not, Your Majesty?" Athos asked.

"Not really," Louis admitted.

"But . . . you're the king," Greg ventured. "You can do whatever you want. You, more than anyone, can have some fun."

Louis sighed tiredly, sounding much older than his years. "Fun? Let me tell you about my life. When I was nine, my father was assassinated right in front of me. I've had to run the entire country ever since. The Germans, the English, the Spanish, and the Italians are constantly threatening war. There are about twenty noble factions within France at odds with one another as well. My mother and my half brother are planning separate coups to overthrow me. And I'm being forced to marry a girl I've never met—whose language I don't even speak—solely for political reasons. Does that sound like fun to you?"

Greg shook his head, embarrassed. "I'm very sorry," he murmured, and meant it.

"With all due respect, Your Majesty," Porthos chimed in, "I'd be happy to offer my services to rectify the situation. As you said, I'm quite good at having fun. We could sneak you out of here one night, attend a masquerade ball. . . ."

Louis shook his head sadly. Greg was stunned: He

actually felt bad for the king of France. The old servant entered again, approached Louis, and spoke softly in his ear. Louis waved him back toward the door and then fixed his gaze on Greg.

"Now let's see what we can do about your parents."

"You mean . . . You think they're innocent?" Greg asked hopefully.

Louis lifted his shoulders and sat up straight. "I think we should at least investigate the possibility of their innocence."

Greg breathed out a sigh. For the first time since being sucked into the past, it seemed as if he might actually have a chance at saving Mom and Dad. "Thank you, Your Highness. Thank you for understanding."

"It is nothing." Louis snapped his fingers. "I've asked the head of my guard, Dominic Richelieu, to join us."

The servant opened the door, allowing Richelieu into the room.

Greg turned. His throat caught. All the warmth in his body evaporated.

He knew Richelieu. Only when Greg had met the man, he'd called himself Michel Dinicoeur.

FOURTEEN

G REG COULDN'T BELIEVE HIS EYES.

It wasn't simply the surprise that Dinicoeur was also Richelieu. Dinicoeur also looked different. It was obviously the same man, and yet . . . As impossible as it was, he seemed *younger* somehow. His face was smoother, his hair longer, and there was something else strange about him, though Greg was too stunned by his sudden arrival to figure out what it was. . . .

Dinicoeur was surprised to see Greg in the king's chambers as well—though he seemed even more startled by the presence of Athos, Porthos, and Aramis. It seemed to Greg that something like recognition flashed in Dinicoeur's eyes. A cruel smile crossed his face, as though he were almost pleased by the turn of circumstance. "Guards!" he yelled.

Four soldiers flooded through the door at his command.

"Arrest these boys at once," Dinicoeur ordered. "Take them directly to La Mort."

The soldiers turned to the king for verification.

Louis looked to Dinicoeur, baffled.

"He is a traitor!" Dinicoeur exploded, thrusting a finger at Greg. "Nothing he says can be trusted!"

Greg knew then that they had to escape. Whoever Dinicoeur was or was pretending to be, he had the king's trust. "The drapes," he whispered to his friends.

The other boys instantly understood. They whirled around and yanked on the window coverings. The huge swaths of fabric, big as the sails of a ship, tore free from the wall. The soldiers scattered—but not quickly enough. The drapes billowed over them, plunging them into darkness. Porthos grabbed a vase off its decorative pedestal and then heaved it through the window, shattering the glass with a deafening crash.

"I can pay for that," he told Louis.

The king didn't seem to hear. He'd crouched on the floor, covering his ears and squeezing his eyes shut. Porthos dove out the window and onto the scaffolding that surrounded the palace—trailed by Athos and Aramis. As Greg followed, Dinicoeur caught him by the arm. *With his right hand.* Even though his life was at stake, Greg couldn't help but stare at it in shock. When Greg had shaken that hand in the twenty-first century, it was prosthetic. Now it was flesh and blood.

Dinicoeur smiled at Greg's confusion. He clenched Greg's throat in his other hand and squeezed. "Perhaps I'll spare you the agony of La Mort and simply end your life now," he hissed.

In response, Greg kicked Dinicoeur in the groin.

Dinicoeur gasped and toppled back into the king's chamber, falling on top of the heaving sea of drapes. Greg charged after his friends down the planks of the scaffolding, leaping over mounds of mortar and piles of stone. Porthos, Aramis, and Athos were well ahead of him. In a panic, Greg glanced over his shoulder. *Nuts.* The guards had freed themselves and were scrambling out the window.

They were in the huge central courtyard of the palace. Ahead, the scaffolding ended abruptly at a vast archway that led to the street. Porthos, Aramis, and Athos slid down a ladder to the ground and held it steady as Greg nimbly followed. Together, the four ripped the ladder from its moorings and shoved it away as the soldiers reached for it. It smashed to bits on the ground, stranding Dinicoeur's men twenty feet above them. Dinicoeur himself was nowhere to be seen.

For the briefest instant, Greg felt relief, until the soldiers started shouting for help.

An entire platoon poured out of a door on the opposite end of the courtyard. Porthos led the way through the archway toward the front door, where their horses were still tethered, guarded by one of the sleepy-looking teenage soldiers. Athos slipped up behind him and snatched his sword from his scabbard. The young soldier took one look at the blade and fled.

As the boys untied the reins and climbed astride the horses, Greg caught a glimpse of someone watching them from a window upstairs. Milady de Winter. *Where has she been?* he wondered. Had she fended off Valois and Dinicoeur for as long as possible . . . or had she led Greg and the others straight into a trap? He noticed the other boys staring at her as well. Athos's and Porthos's eyes narrowed in suspicion, while Aramis broke into a huge smile.

"Forget her," Athos hissed. "Before all her help is for naught." He smacked Aramis's horse on the rear, sending it charging into the city. Greg kicked at his own horse and leaned forward. The sudden speed nearly threw him from the saddle. The deafening thunder of hooves filled his ears as the wind whipped through his hair, his bones rattling with the rapid up-and-down motion.

Greg clung tightly to the reins. He knew how to handle a steed at a full gallop, but always on a dirt track specifically tailored for riding. Now he found himself steering an unfamiliar horse through crowded and uneven cobblestone streets while mounted soldiers bore down on him.

He had no idea where he was going. But Porthos and Athos seemed sure of themselves, so he just followed them. Nearby, Aramis looked as if he were having as tough a time as Greg. Then again, he was neither royalty nor militia, so he was unused to horseback riding.

Greg fought the temptation to look back at the soldiers pursuing them. He couldn't stop thinking about Michel Dinicoeur. How could the man from the future *also* be Dominic Richelieu? He'd only come back through time when Greg had, two nights before. He couldn't have invented an entirely new identity . . . unless that *wasn't* the first time Dinicoeur had visited the past. But that was impossible; Dinicoeur hadn't been able to pass through time *until* he'd gotten his hands on Greg's mother's crystal. And what about his hand? How had it grown back?

Upon hurtling around a corner, Greg spotted one of the city gates looming ahead: two thick stone towers with a narrow gap between them, spanned by a stone arch— and manned by four sentries. Two of the sentries readied their crossbows while the other two raced down the stairs toward the massive winch that controlled the iron portcullis. Greg gulped. Once the portcullis spikes hit the ground, his exit would be cut off. Or worse, he'd be impaled. . . .

Up by the gates, Athos leaped off his horse while it was still moving, whipped out his sword, and fended off the guards. Porthos and Aramis began to rein their own mounts, but Athos waved them on and they thundered through the gate behind Athos's steed.

Greg allowed himself one tiny glance over his shoulder as his horse approached Athos. Bad idea. Valois was leading the charge and closing the gap. Greg could feel the ground trembling from the horses' hooves. He faced forward, galloping faster. A crossbow from the sentries atop the gate whistled past his ear.

Immediately ahead, Athos fended off the guards a final time, then whirled around and kicked the lever that locked the winch in place. The winch spun wildly, unspooling the chain around it and the portcullis hurtled toward the ground. In a fluid move, Athos grabbed the reins of Greg's horse and leaped on its back, seating himself behind Greg. The horse never broke stride. It charged under the arch just as the gate thudded into place behind them.

Valois's horse whinnied in fear and skidded sideways, slamming the soldier into the iron bars.

"*Au revoir*, Valois!" Athos taunted. "Once again, you have failed in your duties."

"Laugh now!" Valois spat back. "But this isn't the last you've seen of me."

Up ahead, Porthos laughed. "The thought of seeing your face again *is* terrifying."

The boys spurred their horses and galloped away into the countryside. As thrilled as Greg felt that they'd escaped with their lives (for the time being), he didn't find much humor in Porthos's joke. Because Greg *was* terrified at the idea of seeing Valois again. And now that Dinicoeur had reappeared, Greg had a creeping suspicion he would.

 # FIFTEEN

As the sun set over the rolling hills and fields, Porthos led the way to his family's "country residence." Greg was a little more familiar with his surroundings by now . . . and he was almost able to laugh at the location. Four hundred years later, the palatial gardens and stables would be buried under several thousand tons of concrete to form the runways of Charles de Gaulle Airport. But in 1615, a turreted castle stood in place of a control tower.

Porthos's home wasn't as massive as the Louvre, but it was less fortresslike. After stabling their horses, Porthos led the four boys through a back entrance into a vast kitchen. Several servants greeted him by an open hearth at its center. They informed Porthos his parents had left for a few days, touring the far-flung portions of their land, which extended, Greg learned, halfway to Belgium. Porthos shrugged this off as if it happened all the time, then led the boys through a narrow passageway. Greg soon found himself seated at a table with the others in front of a roaring fireplace—devouring fresh bread, cheese, and sausage.

"Something's not right here," Porthos told Greg. "Richelieu *knew* you. I could tell when he entered the king's chambers. He was surprised to see you, and he immediately demanded our arrest."

Greg nodded. "I know. But, even stranger, he recognized all of you, too."

The other boys exchanged confused looks.

"That's impossible," Aramis stated. "I've never seen him before in my life."

"Neither have I," Porthos said.

"I've spent a year in the militia *trying* to get Richelieu to recognize me," Athos added. "But I never have. I can guarantee you: The man has no idea who I am."

Greg shrugged. "Maybe he didn't before, but he does now. I saw it in his eyes. He knew who all of you were. He seemed even more surprised to see you than me."

"Nonsense," Aramis argued. "He was looking at you the whole time. How is it that the head of the king's guard knows a boy from Artagnan who arrived here only two days ago?"

"Because Richelieu is *also* Michel Dinicoeur," Greg replied.

The boys gaped at him, trying to comprehend. Greg had expected this. He'd put a lot of thought into how much he could reveal about Dinicoeur—without revealing that *he* was from the future, too.

"I don't understand," Porthos admitted.

"He introduced himself to my family as Michel Dinicoeur," Greg explained. "He's the man who stole from us, who we followed to the palace, and who condemned my parents to death. But it wasn't until he entered the king's quarters that I discovered his true identity."

Aramis's expression hardened. "D'Artagnan, I think it's time you owned up about what he stole from you."

Greg bit his lip. He'd never heard Aramis sound so impatient or exasperated. "I told you . . . it's a cherished family heirloom."

"Yes, but *what is it?*" Aramis demanded. "I'd like to know the full story."

"It's a piece of jewelry. An extremely valuable necklace. In fact, it's the most valuable thing my family owns." Greg felt that wasn't too much of a stretch. Even if the crystal wasn't expensive, if it could get his family back to the twenty-first century, it was worth more than all the gold in the world.

Aramis furrowed his brow. "Even if Richelieu is a thief, why would he journey all the way out to Artagnan to steal a piece of jewelry? If he wanted to steal something, there are no doubt hundreds of jewels in the palace."

Greg frowned, unsure what to say. That was an excellent question. Thankfully, Athos answered for him.

"Because if he stole from the palace and got caught, he'd end up on the gallows. But look what happens when Richelieu steals from some noble yokels no one in Paris knows: He has the clout to condemn them to death and no one bats an eye."

"Very clever, when you think about it," Porthos chimed in. "He could be robbing the countryside blind. But because of his position here, no one can touch him."

"That's right," Greg said quickly. "That's probably why he did it. I mean, that's probably why he singled out my family, you know?"

Athos and Porthos nodded.

"I suppose you're right," Aramis said, though Greg could tell from his tone he still wasn't convinced.

"I think we should keep an eye on Richelieu," Greg said.

"And I think we should worry about one thing at a time," Athos replied. "You don't think freeing your parents from La Mort is enough to do? Richelieu and Valois have both seen all four of us. It won't be hard to figure out we're the ones who broke into Richelieu's office, and once he realizes what's missing . . ." Athos didn't bother to finish.

"Richelieu's no fool," Aramis said with a grimace. "He's probably already figured out our plans for La Mort. To break into the prison now is suicide."

Greg felt himself go pale.

"Not necessarily." Porthos stared pensively into the roaring flames. "There are always ways to turn a man's suspicions against him. Believe me. We won't know how to play this game—or even if we *need* to play this game— until we know what Richelieu is up to. Which means D'Artagnan is right. We need to keep an eye on him."

"How?" Greg asked. "Aramis just said we have other things to do."

"Well, it will take all four of us to *conduct* the break-in, but perhaps not to plan it," Porthos said. "Let's see the architectural plans."

Greg pulled the parchment from the folds of his shirt and laid it on the table while servants cleared the dishes.

Porthos smiled. "Now that we have *this*, we only need to combine Aramis's brains with my knowledge of the prison. We can hatch the plan while you and Athos investigate Richelieu."

Aramis frowned. Greg could tell that he wasn't excited about spending a lot of time alone with Porthos, whom he considered lazy and pampered. "You promise to actually help me?" Aramis asked dubiously. "You won't just goof off while I do all the work?"

"I swear it." Porthos took a knife and pressed the blade

against his hand. "I'll even do it on a blood oath, if you'd like."

Aramis turned slightly green. "Thank you, no. Your word is good enough."

Porthos smiled and rubbed his hands together. "Then let's get to work."

The sun had set by the time Greg and Athos got back to Paris. Athos recommended that they tie their horses several hundred yards from the Bastille gate in order not to attract attention. Peasants arriving on such fine horses might have raised eyebrows among the guards. They'd also borrowed some of Porthos's servants' filthier and more ill-fitting clothes.

The moon was high in the sky when the two boys reached a spot along the Seine where they could scope out the Louvre.

Finding a place where a kid could just hang out and not look suspicious turned out to be harder than Greg had expected. There weren't any benches or parks; there weren't even any restaurants. As Greg recalled from his one semester of European history, the first restaurant wouldn't be opened in Paris—or all of Europe, for that matter—for another fifty years. (And it would serve only one dish: sheep's feet simmered in wine sauce. Gross.) There *were* a few pubs. Anyone of any age could drink alcohol, but neither boy had ever had so much as a sip of wine before . . . and it probably wasn't smart to make this their first time.

This particular stretch of riverside road was completely deserted, but Athos had an idea how to remain inconspicuous. He snapped two long branches off a tree and tied some string to the ends. Then he and Greg sat on the bank of the Seine, pretending to fish. Greg couldn't imagine anyone would ever eat anything that came out of the putrid river, but Athos pointed out that beggars literally couldn't be choosers.

"But you've all turned the river into a cesspool!" Greg exclaimed.

"Where else would you have us put our waste?" Athos asked. "In our homes?'

Greg didn't have an answer for that. Trying to explain a sewage treatment plant to Athos would bring up more questions than it answered—and to be honest, it wasn't as if people in the future were doing a great job keeping rivers clean. Still, the river reeked. Athos appeared not to notice, but Greg's stomach pitched queasily. He tried to breathe through his open mouth. It didn't help. He could almost *taste* the filth.

"You don't like Paris, do you?" Athos asked.

Greg blanched. "Sure I do. . . ."

"You lie. I've seen the way you look at it, the way you wrinkle your nose in disgust. You believe the entire city is a cesspool, not only the river."

"It's just . . . well, the city isn't quite what I expected," Greg admitted.

"There are many who say it is the greatest city in the world," Athos said.

"I know. And it probably is. I guess I miss home."

Athos nodded. "That I can understand. Do you have a fiancée back there?"

Greg nearly dropped his stick into the water. "You're joking, right?"

"Hardly. Remind me: How old are you?"

"Fourteen," Greg answered.

"Exactly. You're getting on in years. The king is fourteen and *he's* getting married."

Greg felt his face getting hot. He was glad they were far from the nearest torchlight. "I thought that was only for political reasons."

"It's also the right time. What age do people get married in Artagnan?"

"Uh, well, in their twenties, mostly. Sometimes even later than that."

"You mean, when they're thirty? They're almost dead by then!" Athos laughed. "What could everyone possibly be doing for all that time if they're not raising a family?"

Greg stared out over the river. The thing that bothered him most about time travel was the constant lying. He wanted to be honest, to tell Athos—or anyone—about the future. About all the things that were different: schools, cars, airplanes, restaurants, refrigerators, cell phones, computers, hospitals, flush toilets . . . The list went on and on. Maybe Athos would believe him; maybe he'd even be impressed. But not everyone would. Once the secret was out, he wouldn't be able to control how people reacted.

"Are *you* engaged?" Greg finally asked.

Athos sighed with a sad smile. "Me? My family doesn't have the means to arrange a wedding. We had hoped my military service would make me a better prospect, but . . . that seems to be over. I don't know how I'll tell my parents about it."

"Perhaps there's still a way to get you reinstated," Greg offered. All at once he felt terrible. He'd been so focused on rescuing his parents that he hadn't stopped to consider all the havoc he'd been causing among the lives of his new friends . . . kids who'd risked everything to help a perfect stranger.

"After what we did today?" Athos mused. "Not very likely."

"Then why are you helping me? If it's ruining the prospects for your life—"

"Because it's the right thing to do. My father might not have had much, but he did give me a code of honor." Athos absently tapped his fingers on his fishing pole. "Maybe it was foolish of me, but I thought *someone* in the military would respect that. Someone would prize skill over birthright. I know it's heretical to say it, but sometimes this whole class system just seems *wrong* to me."

Greg nodded. "For what it's worth, I agree with you."

Athos mustered a tired grin. "You say things that are better left unsaid, D'Artagnan. Is everyone as plainspoken where you come from?"

"Yes," Greg said. He decided right then and there to tell the truth as much as he possibly could. "The class system *is* wrong. And it won't be like this forever. Someday, people will be judged on their merits—how smart or talented they are—instead of who their parents are. They'll be able to *choose* who they want to marry instead of having weddings arranged for them. And kings and queens won't matter anymore. People will elect the real leaders. . . ." Greg trailed off, realizing Athos was staring at him in shock.

"I had no idea," Athos said. "You *really* don't like the monarchy."

"Well, I . . . um, that's not exactly true. The king seemed nice. You know, for someone who . . ." He wanted to say, *Someone who has led a completely sheltered life and probably has no real friends.* But that would definitely be a little too over the top.

"Someone who was picked by God himself to rule France?" Athos finished for him. "Do you expect the people could pick someone better, D'Artagnan?"

Greg swallowed, staring back out at the river. "I know it sounds crazy."

"I didn't say that," Athos continued. "It sounds . . . well, different. I've never heard such ideas before."

"Forget I mentioned them."

"Why? They're very interesting. Especially this idea of choosing the girl you want to marry . . ." Athos shot a wistful glance at the stars.

Greg smiled. "Athos? Is there a girl you like?"

"Yes. But it could never happen. Maybe in your fantasy world, but not this one."

"Who is she?"

"It's a long story."

"We have a long night ahead of us," Greg pointed out.

"No, we don't." Looking past Greg, Athos dropped his makeshift fishing pole into the water and leaped to his feet. "Richelieu is on the move!"

Greg followed Athos's eyes. Sure enough, Richelieu had emerged from the palace. Greg had only a moment to glimpse the man's demonic face before he pulled a cowl over his head. Instead of his formal uniform, he wore a dark cloak, like that of a monk. He moved stealthily, avoiding pockets of torchlight, as though trying not to draw attention.

"Wearing a disguise? He's definitely up to something," Athos whispered.

Neither Greg nor Athos uttered another peep as they trailed Richelieu through the narrow, twisting streets. Richelieu seemed to be on his guard, but it wasn't hard for the boys to stick to the shadows and go unnoticed.

Eventually he reached a tiny church in a dark alley. It was nowhere near as grand as Notre Dame. Greg might have mistaken the place for a peasant's home had it not been for the large cross over the entrance.

Richelieu passed through the wooden doors, which creaked loudly. Greg frowned. There was no way the boys could follow without making an equally loud noise. Athos jerked his head toward the stained-glass window on the side. One of the panes was broken. They tiptoed up to it and peered inside.

Inside, Richelieu felt comfortable enough to drop his cowl. The church was empty except for a lone monk, who knelt at the small altar in prayer. Richelieu approached, lit a candle, and kneeled beside him. The monk turned. In the light from Richelieu's candle, the boys caught a glimpse of a profile under the heavy black hood.

Both gasped in surprise.

The monk wasn't a monk at all . . . or even a man.

It was Milady de Winter.

SIXTEEN

GREG STRAINED HIS EARS TO CATCH EVEN A WISP OF WHAT Richelieu and Milady were saying. But their voices were too hushed. He could only wait. . . .

The conversation lasted less than two minutes. At the end, Richelieu handed Milady a piece of paper that she tucked beneath her cloak. Greg thought he caught a glimpse of a formal wax seal. She stood and headed for the door.

"Follow her!" Athos hissed. "I'll stay on Richelieu."

"*You* don't want to follow her?" Greg asked, baffled.

"Richelieu knows you and wants you dead. And I would

guess that he's far more dangerous than she is. I can handle him. I doubt you can."

That made sense—and besides, there was no time to debate. Greg scurried after Milady, careful to maintain a distance of at least half a block between them. She moved furtively, glancing over her shoulder and pausing every now and then, as if to listen for footsteps. Greg froze when she did, falling into a rhythm. Milady crossed the Seine by way of the Île de la Cité—avoiding the lively Pont Neuf—then quickly cut through the southern part of Paris toward a low-walled compound.

As far as Greg could tell from his distant vantage point, it was almost like a city within a city. He even thought he heard the cluck of chickens and bray of horses on the other side, as if there were a farm inside. Milady cased the street one last time to make sure she was alone, then knocked on a small wooden door. Someone opened it immediately, as though they'd been waiting for her. Once the door closed, Greg heard a bolt slide and click on the other side, locking it tight.

So . . . he wouldn't be following her *that* way. Fortunately, the stone was rough enough that, with his rock-climbing skills, he could scale it. Besides, the walls didn't seem built for defense so much as to provide solitude. It wasn't a difficult climb, maybe twenty feet or so. In less than half a minute, Greg reached the top and peered into the compound.

As he'd surmised, there was a small farm: pigsties, chicken coops, stables, and goat pens—as well as a large vegetable garden and several fruit trees. On the far side, right next to the city wall, was a plain white tower, virtually unornamented except for a few stained-glass windows. Though that might not mean it was a church. Greg knew that stained glass was a lot easier to make than clear glass, and a lot sturdier as well. Surprisingly, the compound had its own gate in the city wall itself, one that didn't appear to be controlled by the king's soldiers.

At that moment, its portcullis was being winched open by someone in a cloak.

At first, Greg assumed it was Milady, but when he caught a glimpse of beard, he realized that he was looking at an actual monk. *Aha.* This place was probably a monastery. He inched up farther, preparing to swing his legs over the top of the wall, when the clatter of hooves caught his attention. A horse charged out of the stable, a cloaked figure astride it. Greg couldn't see the face, but given that slight build, he was sure it had to be Milady. The horse thundered across the compound, through the gate, and into the countryside beyond.

The monk quickly winched the portcullis shut and locked it.

Greg slithered back down the wall, dejected. There was no way he could have followed Milady without a horse. Still, he'd failed. He had a zillion unanswered questions.

What was Milady doing for Richelieu? Who were these monks? And if Richelieu was up to no good, why were they working with him? Hopefully Athos was having better luck.

All at once, a very disturbing thought occurred to Greg.

He had no idea how to get in touch with Athos.

They'd never considered that they might split up, so they'd never made a plan about what to do if that happened. Back in modern times, Greg never gave much thought to getting in touch with people because everyone had a phone.

So think like someone in 1615, Greg told himself. Athos would eventually head back out to Porthos's family estate, right? Of course he would. Except the idea of making that long journey now—late at night, exhausted and alone—without Athos to protect him against thieves or wild animals or whatever else . . . no way. Notre Dame was far closer. Greg could see the towers less than a mile away. Better to take his chances and sneak back into Aramis's garret, and then return to Porthos's residence at sunrise.

As Greg cut back through the city, his gloomy mood grew worse. It was the first time he'd been alone since he'd met Aramis. In addition to being scared, he was overcome with guilt. His parents were still locked in La Mort, having no idea what had happened to him or that he was planning to rescue them. All *they* knew was that they were condemned to death in less than two days' time. Time was running out.

Worst of all, Greg couldn't help but doubt himself. He'd been lucky to make allies—he couldn't discount that—but of all the boys, he was by far the weakest link. Aramis had the brains. Athos had the skills. Porthos had guile and confidence. Greg brought nothing to the table. He was clueless about how to navigate medieval France without the help of the others. If anything, he was probably a *threat* to the mission of rescuing his parents.

By the time he reached Notre Dame, he felt useless and miserable.

The wall around the cathedral garden was even easier to scale than the wall of the monastery. Once inside, Greg remembered how to get to Aramis's room, though he proceeded slowly. The ancient wooden floorboards threatened to squeak with every step. How could he explain himself if he woke the clergy who lived here? He finally made it up to the garret—and, sagging, pushed open the door. In the moonlight, he could see his original clothes still folded neatly where he'd left them. . . .

Out of the corner of his eye, he saw something move.

Greg whirled around as his attacker sprang from the shadows. Reflexively, he crouched: shoulder cocked, feet braced. Something hard thumped Greg on the head. He winced in pain as he and his assailant tumbled to the floor. Greg rolled away and hopped to his feet, slightly dizzy. He was about to pounce when his opponent slipped into a shaft of moonlight. "Aramis?" Greg gasped.

"D'Artagnan? Is that you?" Aramis dropped the thick book he'd used as a weapon, embarrassed. "What are *you* doing here?"

"It was too late to go back to Porthos's place," Greg explained. His adrenaline had spiked and his heart was still racing. "Why aren't *you* there?"

"Porthos and I were working on the plan, but we realized we needed to take another look at La Mort." Aramis stared at the floor. "And once we'd ridden all the way back this way, I thought I ought to come back here for the night. I need to show myself around here tomorrow so the priests don't start wondering what I'm up to."

Greg's breathing began to slow. "Then why'd you attack me?"

Aramis looked up. "No one ever comes up here. And no one in the cathedral is ever up this late. So when I heard you coming up the stairs, I thought it was an intruder. We've earned our share of enemies lately." He pursed his lips. "Where's Athos?"

"We had to split up. He was following Richelieu and I—"

"Wait!" Aramis interrupted, his eyes widening in confusion. "Athos was following *Richelieu*?"

"Yes. Why? That was the plan, wasn't it?"

Aramis began to pace the room. "Yes, but . . . When was Athos following him?"

"Well, we both were, to begin with. We saw him leave the Louvre about two hours after the sun went down—"

"No, that's not possible."

"Why not?"

Aramis stopped pacing and met Greg's gaze. "Because I saw Richelieu at La Mort at the exact same time."

SEVENTEEN

"THAT CAN'T BE," GREG SAID. "YOU MUST HAVE THE TIME wrong."

"I don't," Aramis replied, flopping into the straw bed. "Porthos and I decided to go to La Mort shortly after you and Athos left. We arrived there right at sunset and stayed for several hours. We were just about to leave when we saw a boat departing from the prison, so we stayed hidden until after it docked on the shore. Richelieu was on that boat. Which means that he'd been inside La Mort the entire time we were watching. So there's no way you and Athos could have seen him at the Louvre at that time. Unless there's a secret passage from the prison to the mainland. But even then, it wouldn't make sense."

Greg nodded, exhausted. "You're right. Unless Richelieu has a twin." The words popped out of his mouth before he'd even had a chance to think about what he was saying. But a thought began to dawn on him. . . .

"Impossible," Aramis replied. "The only brother Dominic Richelieu has is the cardinal, and they don't look a thing a like."

All of a sudden, Greg was wide awake again. "Can you be sure, though?"

Aramis blinked. "That family couldn't have kept a twin a secret. They're too closely connected to the monarchy."

"Then maybe they had the king's help," Greg said. "Because Michel Dinicoeur doesn't have a right hand, and Dominic Richelieu does. They're two different people!"

Aramis's eyes went wide. "Michel Dinicoeur is missing a hand? Why didn't you tell us that before?"

"Because it sounded crazy," Greg admitted. "But now, everything makes sense." He hesitated. "Well, a *little* more sense, at least. . . ."

"D'Artagnan, tell me," Aramis said. "What did you observe Richelieu—or Dinicoeur—doing tonight?"

Greg related the details of his evening, how he and Athos had trailed Richelieu to a church, then how they'd split up when they'd spotted him connecting with Milady, and how he'd tailed Milady to the southern part of town. Aramis's eyes clouded at the mention of Milady's name, but he said nothing. When Greg began to describe the monastery, however, Aramis sat up excitedly.

"Wait!" he interrupted. "That's the Abbey of Saint-Germain-des-Prés!"

Greg paused. He knew the name from his own time. Saint-Germain was one of the most famous neighborhoods in modern Paris. Back before everything had gone wrong, his parents had been planning a trip there—in the twenty-first century, Saint-Germain was more famous for its cafés and shopping than its religious roots.

"Is it . . . I'm not sure how to ask this," Greg began. "Does the abbey answer to the king? It looks like a city within the city, and it has its own entrance in the wall."

"You're sharp, D'Artagnan," Aramis replied. "The abbey has been around for over a thousand years, so it's older than most of Paris. Saint-Germain lives by its own laws. It owns a great many fields outside the city, and it maintains its own port of entry."

Greg nodded. It made sense: *des prés* meant "of the meadows" in French. Funny: He'd wondered why such an urban neighborhood, smack in the middle of Paris, would have such an incongruous name. "I guess the next question would be: Is the abbey friendly with the king?"

Aramis brushed a hand through his stringy hair. "I'd always thought so. But now, I wonder. If Richelieu wanted

Milady to do something for Louis, he would have just sent her from the Louvre. But why would he ask a handmaiden to do anything for him, unless it was something he'd prefer to keep hidden?"

Greg's thoughts raced but ended up down a bunch of blind alleys. He had no idea what Milady could have been doing. He rubbed his bleary eyes and suddenly noticed how grubby his hands were. Yuck. He would do anything for a bath—or even a sink. And Notre Dame was supposed to have the height of modern plumbing. . . . Thinking about the cathedral, an idea struck him. "Do you think she's on a mission for the church?" he asked.

"I don't know what to think." Aramis sighed. "Unlike his brother, the cardinal, Dominic Richelieu has never seemed to be a man of God to me. And yet, here he is, in league with Saint-Germain *and* Milady de Winter. I can't imagine *she'd* be up to anything untoward. Not without being forced into it, at least."

Greg wasn't so sure. Richelieu hadn't threatened Milady in any way—at least not as far as Greg could tell. He decided not to argue the point, however. Aramis clearly had his own opinions of Milady, and Greg had a hunch he wouldn't be able to change them. "Did you see Richelieu— or Dinicoeur—do anything at La Mort?" he asked.

Aramis shook his head. "No. We saw him leave the prison and get in a carriage. It seemed to be headed toward the city."

Greg chewed his lip. "Did you learn anything about the prison?"

"I'm sorry, D'Artagnan." Aramis drew in a quavering breath. "About rescuing your parents . . . you see, we do have some ideas about what to do once we're inside. It's getting to the prison itself that's impossible. You might be able to swim, but the rest of us still have to reach the island as well. Even if we could somehow find a boat, there'd be no way to approach without the guards spotting us. Even at night, they'd see us coming."

Greg tried to picture the prison in his mind. It was far from shore, but not *that* far. "What if I swam out first?" Greg asked. "Perhaps I could divert the guards until you arrived."

Aramis laughed in response. "Sure. You could tell them you're there, and then while they hacked you to pieces, we could row across. There are a dozen guards posted there at any time. There's no way you could stay alive as long as they knew you were there . . ." Aramis trailed off, suddenly lost in thought.

"What is it?" Greg asked.

Aramis ran to his rickety desk, pulled out the architectural plans of La Mort they'd stolen, and laid them out in the moonlight. He pointed to a small alcove just inside the gate. "According to Porthos, there's a stockpile of gunpowder here. If you could ignite that, we'd have our diversion. In fact, you might even be able to take out the entire gate itself with the explosion. But, no." He clucked his tongue and tapped his finger on the plans. "You'd have to be able to scale the wall."

"I can do that," Greg said enthusiastically.

"You and your tall tales!" Aramis snorted. "How? It's solid rock."

"If it's anything like the wall here, or at Saint-Germain, I can climb it. I've scaled both tonight. Remember how we met?"

Aramis laughed. "Right. You can swim *and* climb walls of rock. I don't suppose you can conjure fire from thin air, as well?"

Greg found himself laughing, too. The exhaustion was making them both a little punchy. "What do you mean?"

"Let's say you perform all the miracles you say you can." Aramis pointed once again at the architectural plans. "You'd need something to ignite the stockpile. And though you can swim the river and scale the wall, I doubt you can do so with a lit torch."

"No. But I could use this." Greg leaped across the room to his pile of clothes and fished through the pockets of his shorts. *Yes!* There it was: the matchbook from the Jules Verne restaurant he'd picked up at his first meal in Paris. Better yet, there were fifty matches inside. He could definitely spare one for a demonstration.

"What in heaven's name . . . ?" Aramis began.

Greg responded by striking a match against the matchbook.

Aramis recoiled in surprise as it exploded in a tiny flame. But then his face burst into a wide, fascinated smile. "This is incredible! How does it work?"

"Uh . . . I have no idea," Greg admitted. "But if we wrap these matches in something waterproof while I swim over, I can set anything you need on fire." He touched the lit match to a candlewick, illuminating the room.

Aramis laughed. "D'Artagnan! This is unbelievable! You can swim, climb walls, *and* make flames. I think, thanks to you, we may save your parents yet!"

Greg found himself beaming. Maybe he wasn't such a liability, after all. He might have stuck out like a proverbial sore thumb in 1615, but it seemed he did have some useful talents, after all.

Despite the late hour, Aramis was now revved up with excitement. All at once, his eyes zeroed in on the rumpled clothing across the room. In his haste to find the matches, Greg had absently yanked his great-great-grandfather's diary out of the pants pocket and tossed it on top of the pile.

"What is that?" Aramis asked.

"Nothing," Greg said quickly. "Just a book."

Aramis snatched it up before Greg could. "*Just* a book? The handiwork here is so impressive!" He fanned the pages. "This paper is of high quality. And this binding . . .

I've never seen anything like it. The pages aren't tied on, but are attached with some sort of adhesive. Am I right?"

Greg winced. "I guess."

"Where does such a book come from?" Aramis asked.

"Um, I brought it with me." Greg remembered his promise to himself to tell the truth whenever possible. "It's my great-great-grandfather's diary."

"Incredible." Aramis turned the book over in his hands, amazed. "It must be quite old. And yet it's made with a process I've never seen before."

"Yes, well, to be honest, I'm curious about it myself." Greg reached for the diary, but Aramis stepped back and flipped to the first page.

"I can see why." Aramis peered intently at the neat handwriting. "Your great-great-grandfather wrote in English, for one thing. . . ."

"You can *read* that?" Greg cried. *And all this time I've been speaking French?* he wanted to add.

Aramis nodded, studying the page carefully under the candlelight. "I can read English far better than I can speak it. It appears he also used a cipher. . . ."

Greg's jaw dropped. "You can tell that just from *looking* at it?"

"Well, I have some knowledge of ciphers. The church has used them for centuries to protect documents of great importance. As a cleric, I routinely translate them. This appears to be a basic word-skip cipher." He handed the diary back to Greg and tapped the numbers at the top of the page.

Greg squinted at them, baffled.

4/7

"I'm sorry . . . I don't understand," Greg said. "What do you mean by word-skip?"

"Often, if there is a cipher within a book, the first page will give the key to decoding it," Aramis explained. "The key will be hidden at first glance, of course. But consider the date: Four/seven."

"Right. April seventh."

"Well, I was going to say the fourth of July," Aramis muttered, sounding amused. "But perhaps in Artagnan you prefer your dates backward. In any case, the year is missing. Why is that, do you suppose?"

"I have no idea," Greg admitted, though he was secretly glad Jacob *hadn't* written the year. Aramis would have freaked out if he'd seen something like 1885.

"Because it really isn't a date. It's a clue to deciphering the text. In the simplest form, it's telling us to read only the fourth word, then the seventh, then the fourth again, and so on." Aramis plucked a charcoal pencil from the desk and quickly underlined a series of successive words, skipping in clumps of four and seven.

4/7

In any life, there *comes a time for introspection. This* is *my time. Or* more *importantly, to detail what I know.*

> Here *now, perhaps more* than *ever, it is important that*
> *pen* meets *paper. This is* the *task I will undertake for*
> *thine* eyes.

"'There is more here than meets the eyes,'" Greg read, amazed. But the excitement of the discovery faded quickly. "That's all?"

"It's merely another clue," Aramis said. "What else do you find mysterious about this diary?"

"Most of the pages are blank."

"Ah! That *is* interesting." Aramis flipped through the last half of the book, holding the paper so close to the candle that Greg was worried he'd singe it. "Yes, very interesting indeed."

"What?"

"Someone has written on these pages." He handed the book back to Greg. "You can still see the slight indentations and scratches from the writing implement even though it was done long ago."

Greg looked closely and saw the faint scratches. "You still can't read it."

"'There is more here than meets the eyes,'" Aramis quoted with a chuckle.

Greg suddenly understood. "It's invisible ink?"

"Yes." Aramis sniffed the pages. "Of a vinegar base, I believe. Invisible inks are not uncommon in the church either."

"Then—"

"Yes, I can make them appear," Aramis cut in, as if reading Greg's mind. "Though first, I'm going to need a cabbage."

"A cabbage?! Why would you . . . ?" Before Greg could finish the thought, Aramis held a finger to his lips.

Greg fell silent and listened. The wooden staircase leading up to the garret was creaking. *Footsteps.* Aramis dropped to the floor and peered down through a knothole in the wood. "It's Richelieu and his soldiers!" he gasped. "They've found us!"

 # EIGHTEEN

GREG HADN'T BEEN THAT IMPRESSED BY THE HEIGHT OF Notre Dame when he'd first seen it, back in the twenty-first century. For one thing, it was dwarfed by the Eiffel Tower. It was also shorter than half the buildings in New York City. But now that he was skittering across the peaked roof toward the two bell towers, it seemed very tall indeed. One false step and he'd wind up tumbling through the cold Paris night and leaving a dark stain on the street.

Dinicoeur and his men had blocked the stairwell, so

Greg and Aramis had been forced to flee across the roof. In truth, Greg couldn't tell if Dinicoeur or Richelieu was the one in pursuit; he hadn't gotten a look at the hand. Not that it mattered. He was in trouble either way. Aramis had grabbed his most cherished belongings—a crucifix and a vial of holy water—then kicked out the window grating and clambered out onto the ledge. Greg grabbed the diary and the matches and followed.

Fortunately, Notre Dame had been built to allow people to move among every part of it. The cathedral was intended to last for eternity, with the understanding that it would require maintenance. And so Greg and Aramis were able to navigate a tricky exterior network of ledges and open catwalks—and even steps up the steep slant of the roof—though Greg's knees started to feel like jelly. The ledges were thin, the steps were slippery, and every few feet Greg found himself face-to-face with a gargoyle.

From the street, the gargoyles appeared as small as toys, but up here Greg found they were the same size as he was. There were a few angels among them, but most were monstrous: griffins, chimeras, dragons, goat-people, winged monkeys, and bug-eyed homunculi. Half were making hideous faces, sticking out tongues or baring fangs. Greg couldn't imagine what possible reason anyone would have for putting such things on top of a church.

Greg decided to scramble after Aramis on all fours to maintain his balance. It didn't help much. His hands were trembling and his palms were sweaty. As they neared the bell towers, a chunk of the slate roof broke off beneath Greg's feet and skittered down the roof. He watched it sail into the night and disappear. There was a disturbingly long period of silence before he heard it shatter on the ground.

"They're up on the roof!" several voices cried far below.

Greg froze in his tracks.

Aramis glanced over his shoulder. "This way!" he hissed, pointing to the left-hand bell tower. Greg had no choice but to follow. He could see the guards racing to the front door of the cathedral. There was only one way to escape: up.

Upon entering the tower through a tiny window, Greg found himself chasing Aramis up a treacherous, winding staircase. The wood was slick with something slimy . . . and with a shudder, Greg realized what. Hundreds of doves and bats lived in the belfry. They left their droppings wherever they could.

Greg squinted toward the dark ceiling. There in the shadows hung Emmanuel: the gigantic Notre Dame bell. Greg remembered it from French history back at Wellington Prep. In 1615, it was probably the largest bell ever cast, weighing more than fourteen tons. The clapper alone was over a thousand pounds and the size of a wrecking ball. The rope used to ring Emmanuel stretched all the way to the base of the tower.

Greg's feet skidded on the poop-slicked steps, his hands

clutching at the flimsy excuse for a railing. Below, he heard the soldiers enter the bell tower, confer, and then laugh. Seconds later, the stairs began to creak under their booted footsteps.

"Why don't you boys make life easy on yourselves and just give up?" a gleeful voice shouted from the base of the tower.

Valois! Greg shot a panicked glance at Aramis. Neither boy could see a thing in the darkness below.

"If you try to fight, you'll die!" Valois called. "Try anything else and you'll fall to your deaths. You have no choice but to surrender. The king commands it!"

Greg frowned. The king commanded it? How would Louis even know what was going on?

The boys reached the top landing and edged around to the far side of the bell. The walkway ended abruptly, a single spindly rail preventing them from dropping ten stories to the stone floor. Greg could hear the soldiers coming up the stairs quickly below. They were trapped—

"D'Artagnan!" Aramis hissed. "You're good at climbing walls, yes? So I assume you can shimmy a rope?"

In a flash, Greg understood what Aramis was driving at. His jellified knees grew even weaker. "You don't mean—"

"There's no other way out," Aramis hissed.

Greg's grip tightened around the railing. The soldiers were drawing closer. The fragile wooden scaffolding buckled and jerked under their weight. Aramis's idea was risky, but it still seemed far preferable to being caught by Valois or Dinicoeur. "I'll try," Greg agreed.

"Good, then wait for my signal," Aramis instructed. He fell silent after that. The footsteps drew closer. The jeering cries grew louder. The scaffold began to tremble so much that Greg thought it might disintegrate. When Valois's men made it to the highest landing, Greg caught a blade flash in a sliver of moonlight that spilled into the belfry.

"Now!" Aramis whispered, shoving the heavy rope into Greg's hands.

It was nearly four inches thick. Greg clung to its rough surface as tightly as he could. He swung off the landing and over the abyss. . . .

Greg squeezed his eyes shut. His weight on the bell rope made Emmanuel swing.

BONG . . .

The deafening clang of the bell was a painful thunderclap in his ears. Emmanuel slammed into the soldiers on the far side of the landing. Some tumbled back down the stairs; others clung to the railing. Greg wrapped his legs around the rope and slid down, down, down as fast as he could. He felt the rope jolt as Aramis leaped on above him and followed.

It was a pretty brilliant plan, Greg realized. (Well, in spite of the fact that he might suffer permanent hearing damage and severe rope burns . . . But whatever; he could deal.) The rope was their escape route to the bottom, and

Aramis had guessed correctly that the soldiers would be unable to communicate with the bell's racket.

Greg glanced upward. *Uh-oh.* Not every soldier was out of commission. Valois was hacking at the rope with his sword. Several strands frayed with each slice.

"Aramis!" he shouted at the feet descending above him. "Hurry!"

In the echo chamber of the tower, he could barely hear himself. Greg shimmied faster now. His palms and thighs chafed and his arms and legs were cramping, but he ignored the pain. Down he went, hand over hand—and suddenly the rope jolted. Valois must have been close to severing it. Which meant . . . Greg's blood ran cold.

The soldiers have orders to kill me. Period.

No. Wait. That wasn't right. There was no way Dinicoeur or Richelieu could have known Greg had snuck back to Aramis's room. Which meant they were looking for *Aramis.* But how did they know who he was? No one had mentioned his name in the king's quarters; Richelieu had ordered his guards to arrest the boys immediately upon seeing them. Which meant Richelieu *had* recognized the other boys. Somehow he already knew who they were.

Either that, or Milady de Winter had given him the information earlier that night.

Greg tried to shake the thought away. If he couldn't escape, then everybody else would surely end up dead: his parents, for starters . . . although Porthos and Athos might end up dead even sooner. After all, Porthos was easier to find than Aramis. His family was well-known. Had Dinicoeur and Richelieu already tracked him down at his country estate? Porthos and Athos could have been under attack right at that moment. If Dinicoeur was here, posing as Richelieu, then the actual Richelieu could be there, commanding a separate unit of soldiers at the same time. . . .

Greg was so caught up in his thoughts, he didn't notice he'd almost made it to the bottom of the bell tower until he saw the floor just below him. He dropped the last few feet, almost kissed the cold stone in relief . . .

But froze at the sound of steel being unsheathed.

Dinicoeur was waiting for him.

Greg knew it was Dinicoeur, not Richelieu. The fake hand was gloved, but Greg could see how the madman favored the real one. He held his sword in his left as he sprang from the doorway. Greg scrambled away as the blade clanged against the stone but found himself backed against the wall. There was nowhere else to go. Dinicoeur blocked the only exit.

So this is it, Greg thought with a strange detachment.

In the movies, the bad guy always said something dastardly before killing someone. Not Dinicoeur. He simply looked annoyed, as though Greg were keeping him from a dinner date. He lunged forward, slashing with his sword—

Aramis dropped right on top of him. The two tumbled

in a heap on the floor.

Greg noticed the bell rope suddenly go slack.

He dashed into the center of the room, grabbing Aramis and yanking him toward the door. Greg spun to see Dinicoeur stand up, his freakish dark eyes blazing in the shadows. He lifted his sword—

And the thick, massive bell rope, cut free by Valois above, flattened him.

Greg drew in a deep breath. Aramis didn't wait around. He dragged Greg out of Notre Dame and into the Parisian night. Behind them, even with the bell still clanging, they could hear Dinicoeur's scream of rage. Despite their aching legs, neither stopped running. They fled across the closest bridge onto the mainland, not quite knowing where they were going.

Aramis finally skidded to a halt. He had gone pale with fear. "That man," he panted. "He's not Richelieu's twin."

"Of course he is," Greg panted back. "They look exactly alike."

"Even so, he can't be. He's not . . . He's not human."

Greg tried to swallow. "What do you mean?"

"That bell rope is ten stories tall. It might weigh hundreds of pounds. It should have crushed him, falling from that height. But he was still very much alive."

Greg didn't want to believe Aramis. But he had to admit that the cleric had a point. "So what should we do?" he asked.

"Do you still have that diary?"

Greg checked his pocket. His great-great-grandfather's book was still there. "Yes."

Aramis wiped his brow. "Then let's find a cabbage and get some answers."

# NINETEEN

ALTHOUGH IT WAS THE MIDDLE OF THE NIGHT, ALL OF Paris seemed to be awake. Notre Dame's bell usually only rang during the day. The unexpected commotion caused the streets to flood with people. Gossip and rumors spread like wildfire: The city was under siege and the bell was a call to arms; the queen-to-be had finally arrived and the bell was a call to celebrate; the king had died and the bell was a call to mourn.

Aramis and Greg snaked their way through the crowds. They were virtually the only people in the city who weren't staring at the bell towers. Aramis led them across a creek that stank of something other than human waste. Even in the moonlight, Greg could see that the water was discolored from dyes; it was shiny and slick. He also noticed several fish bobbing belly-up.

"Where are you taking us?" Greg asked.

"My uncle's place," said Aramis. "He makes cloth, like my father."

They arrived at a sturdy three-story home that backed onto the poisoned creek. A stout, graying man and woman stood whispering outside—surrounded by half a dozen children ranging in age from toddler to teenager. The entire family, as well as everyone else on the street, had red hands. Greg understood in an instant: They were permanently stained from clothing dye. What a life these people led. . . .

The man lit up upon seeing Aramis.

"Now we'll get some answers!" he exclaimed to the crowd. "This is my nephew! He's a cleric at Notre Dame. He must know what happened."

Aramis shrank as every head swiveled toward him. He hadn't expected to make a speech. "The—the cathedral was attacked tonight," he stammered.

A gasp rippled through the crowd.

"By who?" his aunt asked.

"Thieves seeking to steal from the church. We rang the bell and frightened them off."

The crowd gasped again. Anyone who dared rob the cathedral was certainly doomed to a horrible afterlife. Aramis quickly answered a flurry of questions. No, the thieves hadn't got away with anything. Yes, he was quite sure they weren't Protestants or witches, though they might be enemies of the king. Yes, it had been frightening. In fact, he didn't feel like returning there tonight. Perhaps he could rest in his uncle's home?

"Of course, my boy, you are always welcome here," his uncle replied, and ushered the two inside—away from the prying eyes of the neighbors. The children scurried in after them and shut the door.

The first floor of the house was devoted to the actual making of cloth, with a small storefront. The second seemed primarily used for dining, with a large table and a pot hanging over a wide stone fireplace—whose coals were still hot. The bedrooms were on the third floor. Aramis's uncle and aunt generously offered the boys their bed, but Aramis respectfully declined.

"We're both too shaken from tonight's events to sleep, I think," he said. "If it's all right with you, I think we'd prefer to just sit by the fire."

"Thank you so much for taking us in," Greg added.

The old man and woman peered at Greg curiously, but said nothing and bowed, smiling. "It's nothing," they replied in unison, as if embarrassed to be thanked. They plodded up to the third floor, waving their brood of children after them.

Once the family had vanished upstairs, Greg hissed at Aramis, "Now what's all this about a cabbage?"

"Red cabbage has a mystical property," Aramis explained. He made a beeline for the larder. "When you make water from it, it magically reveals certain invisible inks."

Upon hearing this bizarre pronouncement, Greg had a faint recollection from his seventh-grade chemistry class. Certain vegetable pigments would turn colors when combined with an acid . . . like vinegar. Aramis had smelled vinegar on the diary pages. If the writing was in vinegar ink, cabbage would make it appear.

Greg realized there was no kitchen in the house. What would they have put in it, a dishwasher? A fridge? They didn't even have sinks yet. Instead, there was only a shelf with the family's few plates and utensils and the larder, a large wooden box that doubled as a bench and held the few foods that could last for a while without spoiling.

Aramis dug through it, tossing aside a trove of root vegetables—carrots, parsnips, and leeks—before yanking out a lone red cabbage. Greg chopped the cabbage into fine pieces on the scarred dining table while Aramis filled a flask from the local well. They poured the water into the pot over the fireplace, and when it reached a boil, they dropped the cabbage bits into it.

"This will take a while," Aramis explained. "We have to wait until all the color has been leached from the vegetable."

Greg nodded. He began pacing the hot, stuffy room impatiently.

After fifteen minutes, Aramis found a feather from a previous chicken dinner on the floor and stuck the feather end into the boiling purplish liquid. "Now watch," he murmured.

Greg's eyes widened as Aramis gently brushed a thin sheen of cabbage water over the first blank page of the diary. Almost instantly, the faint lines of the century-old writing began to appear in purple. Aramis then held the paper closer to the fire. The heat sped up the reaction, and the lines darkened.

"Holy cow," said Greg.

Aramis tore out the first page and handed it to him. Then he set to work, painting cabbage water on the next page. Greg read as quickly as he could.

Greetings, dear reader.

You have now discovered the true purpose of this diary: To detail the startling information I have discovered about my family. Before I begin, I feel it is necessary to state for the record that I, Jacob Rich, am of sound mind. The tale that follows may seem outrageous, the ravings of a lunatic.

But I assure you that every word of it is true.

My family emigrated from France to Connecticut in 1642. Our family name was Richelieu. We chose to

*shorten it to Rich upon arrival in Connecticut, in
order to assimilate among the British. We are direct
descendants of Dominic Richelieu, who served in the
court of King Louis XIII and was brother to Cardinal
Armand Richelieu.*

Greg set the paper down, shocked. He felt nauseated. Dominic Richelieu was his direct ancestor. Greg didn't want to believe it was possible, but somehow, he knew it was true. Grandpa Gus had the same dark eyes that Dominic did.

Aramis tore out the next page and shoved it into Greg's hands.

*Dominic was by all accounts a wicked man who used
his position as chief of the king's guard to amass wealth.
Anyone who dared to challenge him was sent to the
gallows. He even plotted against Louis XIII, planning
a coup with the king's deposed half brother, though
mercifully he was thwarted. Ultimately Dominic
framed his coconspirator for the crime. Louis XIII and
Armand Richelieu, then the bishop of Paris, believed his
ruse. Thus Dominic gained even more political power.*

*Dominic also gained powers that were far more
sinister. He dabbled in the Dark Arts, experimenting
with sorcery and witchcraft. His intent as I understand
it was to live forever and enjoy his ill-gotten lucre for all
eternity.*

Of paramount importance for you to know is this: Dominic succeeded in his quest.

Sometime during the Year of Our Lord 1630, he came to possess an ancient relic known as the Devil's Stone. In the mists of antiquity, the crystal had been broken into two pieces. When joined as a whole, the Devil's Stone was rumored to perform many miracles: strike people dead in an instant, turn lead into gold, even open portals in time. I cannot give credence to any of these rumors, though I swear on my own grave: The stone did give Dominic Richelieu the gift of eternal life.

However, Dominic's greed was his own undoing. He couldn't resist one last chance to line his coffers, and framed a small nobleman for consorting with the enemies of France. Dominic intended to send this man to the gallows and take the man's property for himself. But he chose his mark poorly. The noble was the friend of a man named Porthos, who is still known today as one of Alexandre Dumas' famed Three Musketeers.

Dumas claimed that he based the exploits of his Musketeers on real men. I can assure you this is the truth, although this particular tale was unknown to the writer.

Porthos, along with his fellow Musketeers Athos, Aramis, and D'Artagnan, exposed Dominic's plot to the king, who ordered him arrested. Dominic nearly escaped. He tried to use the Devil's Stone to kill the

*Musketeers and might have succeeded had D'Artagnan
not sacrificed his own life to save the others.*

The page slipped from Greg's trembling hands.
D'Artagnan sacrificed his life? Did that mean . . . ? He
couldn't think about that. He didn't know *what* it meant.

Aramis handed the final three pieces of torn diary paper
to Greg. "That's all there is," he murmured. "The rest of
these pages are not inscribed."

Greg devoured the words as fast as he could.

*Before Dominic could attack again, Athos sliced off
the hand in which Dominic held the crystal, rendering
him powerless. The Musketeers quickly subdued him.
Dominic was then stripped of his fortune and sent to
prison in the Bastille, where his gift of eternal life
became his curse.*

*Over the decades, the guards at the Bastille became
aware there was a prisoner who never aged and never
died, and this terrified them so much that they locked
him away in the deepest, darkest pit, avoiding any
contact with him.*

*As for the Devil's Stone, Dominic's own brother,
Cardinal Richelieu, oversaw its ruin. The stone was
cleaved in two once more. The Cardinal chose to disperse
both halves to opposite ends of the earth. I do not know
the fate of one half, though many rumors about it exist:*

It was carried on a ship to the Indian Ocean and tossed overboard in the deepest trench of the sea; it was hauled to the rim of Mount Vesuvius and plunged into the molten lava in the belly of the volcano; it was spirited away along the Silk Road to the farthest reaches of China. Whatever the case, it has never been seen again.

Yet I do know the fate of the other half.

This was entrusted to Dominic's son, a man named Stefan who had been born out of wedlock and who had long since turned his back on his father's nefarious ways. Stefan was dispatched to the New World with a stake of money and a single mandate: He was to take his half of the Devil's Stone and ensure that it never returned to France.

Stefan was my ancestor. Our family profited greatly in the New World, amassing a considerable fortune. In the years hence, there are some family members who have felt that perhaps the stone itself has had a hand in our success. These members have triumphed over others who believed the stone should be destroyed once and for all. Thus it remains in our family to this day under our protection.

I wish I could say that the story ends there, but there is one more twist in this ugly tale. In 1789, the French Revolution began with the storming of the Bastille. Many prisoners were freed. A hideous madman from the deepest pit was rumored to be among them. I cannot *say for sure if this was Dominic, but there is no record of his death at the Bastille.*

As the centuries have slipped by, there are many who have come to believe that the story of Dominic Richelieu is merely a ridiculous bit of family folklore. I can understand their point of view. But I know it to be true. The truth has been passed directly down from Stefan Rich, as has the mission: Protect our half of the Devil's Stone at all costs.

Perhaps Dominic Richelieu still walks the earth, a tormented soul whose plans to live forever in wealth and luxury were dashed by the Musketeers. Perhaps he plots to somehow wreak revenge on their descendants. Whatever the case, it is imperative that he never recover both halves of the Devil's Stone again.

With this, I reach the end of the sad saga of the Richelieu family, save for one last important note. Hopefully, you will never have to confront Dominic, but if you do, there is something else you must know. . . .

At that point, the entry ended. His heart racing, Greg frantically flipped the pages over and then whirled toward Aramis. The cleric shrugged and shook his head. Greg frowned. He couldn't even begin to imagine how to track down the missing message. There was too much else to deal with. But now at least one crucial piece of the puzzle had been solved . . . and in a way, everything else made icoeur wasn't Dominic Richelieu's twin.

ninic Richelieu. Now that he'd traveled back

me, there were two of him.

rse. In the centuries that had elapsed since Dominic was freed from the Bastille, he had created a new identity for himself, and used his knowledge of medieval France to obtain a respected position at the Louvre in modern-day Paris. Biding his time, he'd tracked down the two pieces of the Devil's Stone. Greg didn't know how he'd acquired the first, but as for the second . . . Well, his family had practically handed it right over.

Somehow, the great all-important mission of his family had been forgotten over time. They'd gone from protecting the stone to wearing it as jewelry . . . and finally to dismissing any warnings about bringing it back to France, chalking that superstition up to the delusional silliness of an old man. Now the two halves of the Devil's Stone had been reunited, allowing Dominic to open a portal in time to the past. He'd since teamed up with his younger self.

And they were plotting revenge on the Musketeers.

Last time, Dominic had managed to kill only D'Artagnan. *Him*. After tonight, there was no doubt Dominic and Michel were trying to kill all of them . . . *before* they became the Musketeers. Greg's thoughts returned to Porthos and Athos. Where were they? Were they even still alive?

He glanced at Aramis and discovered that he, too, had been reading the diary pages as they'd slipped to the floor. Now, the cleric stared at him, aghast.

"So, D'Artagnan," he said. "Why don't you tell me where you're *really* from?"

 # TWENTY

THERE DIDN'T SEEM TO BE A POINT TO LYING ANYMORE and besides, Greg was tired of it.

"I'm from the future," Greg admitted. "But you figured that out, didn't you?"

Aramis nodded. He swallowed, inching back toward the fire, as if Greg had a contagious disease. "What's written in the diary . . . It's the only way to explain how Dinicoeur survived in the bell tower tonight. He's immortal. And the only way he could be here now is if he used the Devil's Stone to travel through time. If he could do it, you could do it. It explains much about you. You've never seemed . . . well, quite *right* to me, begging your pardon."

"If it makes you feel any better, I've never seemed quite right to me either," Greg mumbled tiredly. "Even in my own time."

"One part that's puzzling to me . . . ," Aramis began. He ran a hand through his mop of hair. "We become Musketeers? Why do we use muskets? They're a very clumsy form of weaponry."

Greg laughed in spite himself. "I don't know why you're called Musketeers. I'd never thought about it. You're much more famous as swordsmen."

"How far in the future are you from?"

"About four hundred years."

Aramis looked up, stunned. "And people still know of us then?"

"Like my great-great-grandfather wrote, there were books written about you in the nineteenth century. By a man named Alexandre Dumas."

A smile flitted across Aramis's face. "And we're the heroes?"

"Yes."

"So . . . do you know what happens to us?"

"Uh . . . No. Even though Dumas said the stories were based on real people, I'm pretty sure he made up a lot. I mean . . . in the books, the Musketeers already knew one another and were much older when D'Artagnan showed up. Dominic isn't even mentioned and . . ." Greg caught himself. He'd forgotten until now, but Milady de Winter was also a character in the Dumas novels. (Honestly, Greg hadn't paid much attention to the female characters; he was more interested in the fight scenes than any romance.) More importantly, she had been the wife of either Athos or Aramis. To his annoyance, Greg couldn't remember which—but he did recall that she'd betrayed her husband. There was no point to burdening Aramis with any of that, however. Besides, it might not even be true.

"And what?" Aramis asked.

"And besides, now that Richelieu has jumped through time, the story probably isn't the same anyhow," Greg finished. He believed what he was saying—as much for his sake as for Aramis's. "I think he's changing history."

"Is he? Because you followed him . . . and you're D'Artagnan. How could you be in the story if this hadn't happened before?"

Greg realized Aramis had a point. He slumped at the bench beside the kitchen table and rubbed his temples. "I don't know. Maybe I've always been D'Artagnan. Or maybe I replaced the other one somehow. Whatever the case, I'm pretty sure what's happening now has never happened before. . . ." *Otherwise, I'll end up dead very soon*, he was tempted to finish. But he refused to allow himself to believe that.

"Why not?"

"Because Richelieu is *trying* to change history," Greg explained. "He came back to kill you—and the other Musketeers—*before* you could ruin his life. Don't you see? If you're dead, if we're *all* dead . . . then he doesn't go to the Bastille. Then he stays rich and powerful forever."

Aramis nodded. "That's the revenge he plotted over all those years. He found both halves of the Devil's Stone?"

"Yes. You see . . ." The whole crazy story of the past few months tumbled out of Greg's mouth in a garbled rush. How his family had lost everything and then received a mysterious invitation to France from Michel Dinicoeur. How he seemed strange from the beginning, wearing old-fashioned clothes and introducing himself as *I, Michel Dinicoeur*. How he already had the first half of the crystal, but had duped his family into giving up the second. How they'd followed him through the painting into the past . . .

"The stone creates a time portal by making an image come to life?" Aramis asked.

Greg shrugged. "I guess. I've seen it happen only once."

"So it only works in one direction then? You can only go to the past? Because you'd need an image of the future to return to the future." He sighed sadly, averting his eyes. "And there can't be any paintings of the future in the past."

Greg sat upright, suddenly flooded with excitement. "Not necessarily." His cell phone was still back in Aramis's little attic room. (Presuming Valois and his men hadn't destroyed it.) It wasn't as useless as he'd assumed; he'd stored *photos* on it. If the Devil's Stone could make a portrait of the past come to life, perhaps it could also make a photo of the future do the same.

Which meant Greg and his parents could return to the future . . . if they had the Devil's Stone. But they didn't. It had been left in the future. Which meant they'd have to find both halves here in the past if they ever wanted to go home again. And Greg had no idea where to even begin looking for them.

Greg wondered if you could bring the stone through the portal with you. Perhaps that had been Richelieu's original intent: He would only visit the past long enough to kill the Musketeers, then return to the future. If that were the case, then Greg's family had messed up those plans. No wonder Richelieu had been so angry with them after they'd followed him through the painting. Now he was trapped in the past, too. . . .

Greg suddenly realized what Richelieu might be plotting.

"What's wrong?" Aramis asked.

Greg snapped to attention, aware he'd been lost in thought. "Nothing. I was just thinking about Richelieu."

"So was I." Aramis plucked a piece of paper from the floor and scribbled out some words in a diagram. "You're right about Richelieu. He'd been revealing himself to you all along, even in the future."

I, MICHEL DINICOEUR am

DOMINIC RICHELIEU

Greg gasped, amazed. "It's an anagram."

"Precisely," Aramis concurred. "It figures; he's proud and vain. But to the more vital matter: If he came back here to find us and kill us, then in a sense, we've made his work easier for him. We've practically walked right into his hands."

"I know." Greg's shoulders sagged. "I'm sorry. It's my fault. I'm the one who brought you all together."

"It's nothing to be upset about. He would have tracked us down quickly enough anyhow. And now, thanks to you, we're all a team. We don't have to fight him alone—"

"The others!" Greg was suddenly on his feet. "If Richelieu came after you, then he might have—"

"Gone after them. I know. We can only pray that they've escaped. Thankfully, Athos is a far more formidable warrior than either of us—or anyone under Richelieu."

Greg was already halfway to the stairwell. "But even if they've escaped, where do we find them again? No one's home is safe anymore. And we never came up with a place to meet up in case of emergencies. And . . ." He couldn't even finish the thought. Without Athos and Porthos, rescuing his parents from La Mort was impossible. Which meant they might as well be dead.

"We *will* find them." Aramis tried his best to sound confident, even though his voice didn't sound entirely sure. "And we'll rescue your parents. But even after we do that, we'll *still* have to deal with Richelieu. Remember, he has the entire king's guard behind him, while we're only four boys. He's already destroyed our names and reputations. I can't return to Notre Dame. The others can't go to their homes. Soon we won't be safe in the city. And what then? Even if we flee into the countryside, he'll find us sooner or later. What sort of life is that, being on the run forever?"

Greg shook his head, panic seeping through every pore in his body. "So what do we do?"

"Get help from the one person more powerful than Richelieu. The king."

"But the king trusts him," Greg said. "He practically handed us over to Richelieu today."

"Then we'll have to convince him of the truth," Aramis answered firmly. "You said we become Musketeers, and that the Musketeers are the king's private force. So he must trust us eventually."

"But that's in a version of history that may have changed—"

"Whatever the case, Louis XIII is our only hope," Aramis said.

Greg scratched his head through his matted curls. What he would give for a bath, or a shower, or even five minutes alone just to *think*. "We'll never be able to get to him again. We got lucky getting into the Louvre once. This time, Richelieu will be ready for us. The entire king's guard will know who we are. Going back into the palace would be suicide."

"That's why *we're* not going back into the palace. We need an emissary."

Greg realized who Aramis meant. "Milady? But she's working with Richelieu, too! She had a secret meeting with him tonight."

"That doesn't mean she *wanted* to meet with him. She probably had no choice in the matter."

Greg chewed his lip. "Aramis," he said gently. "You don't know that."

"I *do!*" Aramis snapped. "If she'd wanted to betray us before, she would have led us directly to Richelieu. Instead, she brought us to the king. She helped us then and she'll help us now. We can trust her." Aramis quickly gathered his cloak, then strode past Greg down the stairs. "I'm going to find her," he huffed. "If you think it's a bad idea, you're welcome to wait here until I get back."

Aware he'd struck a nerve, Greg ran after Aramis.

It was still dark when they exited the house, though it wouldn't be for long. The sun would be rising within the hour. To Greg's surprise, Aramis headed in the opposite direction of Saint-Germain-des-Prés.

"We don't know if she's coming back into the city that way, but we definitely know where she's going: the palace," Aramis explained. "She's the queen's handmaiden. Even though the queen hasn't moved in yet, Milady has. All servants live at the palace. She'll need to be back before the sun rises. Otherwise, her absence will be noted, which would defeat the entire purpose of a clandestine mission. Let's be quick. We have no time to lose!"

Together, they raced through the predawn streets toward the Louvre. A thick fog had crept up the Seine into the city, shrouding everything in a gloomy mist. As the boys approached the Pont Neuf, they spotted a cloaked figure, scurrying toward the Tuileries.

"Milady!" Greg shouted.

The figure froze. It *was* Milady. Then she began to sprint. The boys ran after her as fast as they could. Their footsteps rang out on the bridge. In the quiet city, they might as well have set off a string of firecrackers.

"Wait!" Aramis called out. "We mean you no harm!"

Milady hesitated on the far bank, peering into the fog, as though she'd recognized Aramis's voice. But at that very moment, someone lunged from the alley behind her and yanked her into it.

"Milady!" Aramis yelled again. He charged headlong toward the alley.

Bad idea, Greg thought, but knew he had no choice except

to chase after his friend. As Greg rounded the corner, he spotted a large man in a cloak trying to subdue Milady. Her cowl had fallen from her head, and the man's hand was clapped over her mouth. Her eyes went wide at the sight of the boys.

No, Greg realized. Not at them. She was looking *past* him.

He spun around—but not quickly enough.

A second assailant grabbed him from behind. Greg tried to struggle, but immediately felt the cool steel of a blade placed against his neck.

"We're taking the girl," his attacker hissed. "Try to stop us and you die."

TWENTY-ONE

G REG FROZE IN FEAR WITH THE BLADE TO HIS NECK, BUT Aramis sprang into action. He snatched a long shaft of splintered wood from a pile of garbage and cocked it over his shoulder like a club. "Lay one finger on either one of those people and I'll cave your heads in."

The person holding Greg gave a gasp of surprise. "Aramis?"

The blade fell from Greg's neck and his attacker stepped from the shadows, revealing his face.

"Athos!" Greg and Aramis exclaimed at once.

The big figure holding Milady pulled back his cowl, revealing himself to be Porthos. "Well, isn't this a pleasant coincidence? Didn't mean to frighten you there. You caught us by surprise."

Greg felt a surge of joy. "You're both alive! We thought Richelieu might have come after you."

"He *did*," Athos said.

"How did you escape?" Greg asked.

"I knew he was coming. Remember, I was keeping an eye on him." Athos then pointed to Milady. "After she left, he stayed in the church, waiting . . . until another man came to meet him there. And you'll never guess who it was."

"His twin," Aramis said.

Athos was stunned. "How did you know?"

"We've been doing some investigating ourselves tonight," Aramis replied.

"So you know they're plotting together," Athos went on. "I watched them hatch a plan in the church. I couldn't hear it then, but it became evident after they left. Each went a separate way, and I chose to follow the one I'd originally been watching. He went directly to the Bastille gate and rounded up the guards. I imagine he told them we had infiltrated the palace that day to assassinate the king. Then he led a party to Porthos's castle so he could kill us in our sleep. Luckily, I deduced where they were heading and rode ahead to get Porthos out before they arrived."

"Not that I couldn't have handled them anyhow," Porthos said, flexing his muscles. Milady rolled her eyes.

"As far as we know, he's still out there, tearing Porthos's residence apart looking for us," Athos said. "There were too many soldiers around for us to get to him, so we had the idea to come here and interrogate his accomplice instead."

"I'm not his accomplice!" Milady snapped.

"Don't lie to me," Athos said sternly. "We saw you with him at the church."

"I had no choice," Milady scoffed. "You have no idea what's going on."

Before Athos could argue, Aramis leaped in to defend her. "She's right. We don't. And as I told D'Artagnan, the fact that she was doing his bidding doesn't mean that she's his accomplice."

"Really?" Athos snorted. "I'd say that doing someone's bidding is the *definition* of being an accomplice."

"Richelieu is a powerful man," Aramis shot back. "She's only a handmaiden. Do you really think she can simply say no to him? Even if she does serve the queen—"

"Shh," Greg interrupted. "We don't want to wake the whole city. We all agree that Milady is worth talking to. And it seems that she wants to tell her side of the story. So let's go someplace quiet to talk to her. Then she can explain everything. How does that sound?"

Aramis and Athos didn't respond right away. They glared at each other.

"I think that's a great idea!" Porthos interjected. "There's a nice quiet church nearby. My family founded it, so they'll take care of us—"

"Hold on a second!" Milady cried. "Don't *I* get a say in any of this?"

"I'm afraid not," Porthos replied. "Seeing as you're possibly in cahoots with an arch-villain who may very well have destroyed my property."

Milady started to argue, but he slapped a hand over her mouth. She squirmed against him and tried to scream.

Porthos frowned at the others. "Can you give me a hand, if you please?"

As wrong as it felt to kidnap a girl, Greg joined the others in hustling Milady through the city. By the time they reached the church, dawn was brightening the eastern sky. Birds had begun chirping. The sounds of crowing roosters echoed across the cobblestones.

The church was locked, but Porthos knocked loudly. The priest in charge was already awake and came quickly. He was a bald man who looked to be in his forties—as portly and ruddy as Porthos himself. He gasped in surprise.

"Sorry to bother you so early, Father," Porthos said. "But I was wondering if we could use the chapel?"

The priest's eyes flickered between Porthos and Milady. "Do you need me to perform a wedding, my lord?"

Porthos laughed. "Uh, no. She's just a friend. We need someplace quiet to talk."

The priest was obviously disappointed. While he seemed extremely curious about what was going on, he asked no questions, instead bowing deferentially. He ushered everyone into the chapel and closed the door behind him, leaving them alone.

Milady finally shook free of their collective grasp. "Keep your hands off me from now on," she warned.

"Fine," Greg said, stepping in front of Athos. "Then just tell us: What was the message Richelieu gave you?"

"How should I know?" Milady said. "It was sealed, so I couldn't read it."

"You don't have to read something to know what it's about," Athos replied. "He might have told you."

"Well, he didn't."

"Whom did you deliver it to?" Athos asked.

"I don't know that either," Milady answered.

"Oh come now!" Athos exploded. "You must have at least *seen* the person!"

"True, but I merely delivered the letter to another messenger. I do not know who he represented."

"Where did you meet him?" Greg asked.

"South of the city," Milady replied. "There is a small inn on the road. I didn't even go inside. He was waiting for me by the stables. I merely handed him the message, turned around, and rode back."

Porthos stepped forward. "What else?"

"Well . . . He did have a strange accent," Milady said, her

eyes flickering toward Greg. "Kind of like yours. But it wasn't the same."

Greg swallowed. "How do you mean?"

"I don't know," Milady admitted. "I've never heard anyone speak like that before. The best I can say is: He wasn't French."

Athos, Aramis, and Porthos shared a look of concern. France wasn't currently at war with any neighboring countries, but Greg knew enough medieval history to recognize that any existing peace was always fragile and short-lived.

"And the Abbey of Saint-Germain-des-Prés?" Aramis asked. "What part do they play in this?"

"The same as I do, I believe." Milady spoke to Aramis in a far less defiant tone than she had used with the others. "Richelieu demanded that they help, so they helped. I don't think they have any agenda other than protecting themselves from his wrath. He sent me there and a friar was waiting. The friar gave me a horse and opened the gate. When I returned, he stabled the horse and let me back into the city."

A rooster crowed close by, perhaps from the church's own courtyard.

Milady's expression grew worried. "I need to get back. If I am not in the palace by sunrise, people will notice my absence."

"You have bigger problems than that right now," Athos stated.

"That is *your* problem," Milady replied. "You want my help? Well, I won't be any help to you if I've been booted out of the palace."

"She's right," Aramis said.

Without a word, Porthos retreated to the rear of the church and waved the others toward him, leaving Milady alone to stew in the front pew.

"I still don't trust her," Athos whispered. "I think she knows far more than she's letting on."

"I don't agree," Aramis countered.

"Your opinion doesn't count," Athos hissed. "You're biased toward her because you're smitten with her."

"And you're biased *against* her because she likes me and not you," Aramis shot back.

Athos's eyes flashed with anger. The rooster crowed again.

"Guys! Please! We're running out of time!" Greg pointed to the east, where the sky was turning pink.

"I apologize, Athos," Aramis offered. "I am tired. And I don't see that we have any choice but to trust her. She's our only way to get to the king, and this is our last chance to see her outside the palace."

"For all we know, she'll go right to Richelieu!" Athos argued.

"Then let's let her do it," Greg heard himself say.

The other boys turned to him, startled. Greg didn't blame them; he was surprised as well. But an idea had just come to him, and he couldn't keep it to himself.

"What are you talking about?" Porthos asked.

"If our greatest fear is that she'll go to Richelieu with any information we give her, then let's use that to our advantage. Let's give her something to tell him." Greg didn't bother to explain himself; he was too worried he'd lose his confidence—however crazy it was. He led the others down the narrow aisle to the front of the chapel and addressed Milady. "Richelieu will come find you today, won't he? To see how your mission went last night?"

Milady stared down at her feet. "I suppose so."

"When he does, tell him we intend to attack La Mort at midnight."

"What?" Milady exclaimed, returning his gaze.

Aramis pulled Greg aside. "Are you insane?" he whispered. "Why would you want Richelieu to know that?"

Greg managed a smile. "Because it's the only way to save my parents' lives."

PART THREE

THE PRISON

TWENTY-TWO

THE STARS SHONE BRIGHTLY OVERHEAD AS GREG approached the Seine with Aramis by his side. Athos and Porthos waited high on the riverbank behind, wary of the water. The moon had yet to rise, and Greg had expected it to be dark. The whole time he'd been in medieval France, the night had always seemed incredibly dark to him, especially compared to the light-polluted cities he was used to. But now that he needed to move under the cover of darkness . . . he could see *everything*.

He'd never really looked at the night sky without light

pollution. There was almost nowhere left in the modern world (other than the middle of the ocean) to see it with such vivid clarity. He'd seen the Milky Way only once or twice in his life, on camping trips. Even then it had only been a diluted pale streak. Now it was a huge, gleaming slash. Once the moon was up, it would be like a spotlight.

Greg's hands began to tremble. La Mort stood in the starlight a quarter mile downstream. Was this really such a brilliant idea? A hundred things could go wrong. All it'd take would be a sentry on the parapet to glance down at the water and spot the telltale ripples of him swimming by—and the entire plan would be ruined. The soldiers would pincushion him with arrows; the other boys would call off the attack . . . and the next morning, his parents would both swing from the gallows.

But if he didn't even *try* to swim, his parents would die for sure.

"You have the matches?" Aramis asked, for what seemed like the hundredth time. He sounded even more nervous than Greg, if that were possible.

Still, Greg checked once again, clutching the satchel Porthos had procured for him: two pieces of leather stitched together tightly so as to be waterproof. Though if water did manage to seep through, the matches were also wrapped in a protective oilskin. The architectural plans of La Mort were in there, too. So were his shoes. He couldn't swim with them, and he'd need dry ones to scale the wall.

Sadly, there wasn't enough room to bring a whole set of dry clothes—although he wouldn't really have the time to change into them anyhow.

"I've got the matches," Greg confirmed.

Aramis hadn't told the others about Greg's miraculous fire-making tools, because explaining where they'd come from might open up a whole new range of questions. And neither Greg nor Aramis felt able to explain any more without ultimately spilling the beans as to where—and when—Greg was really from.

In fact, they'd decided not to tell the other two *anything* they'd learned from the diary: that Dinicoeur *was* Richelieu, that he'd attained immortality, that he'd returned through time to seek revenge on the boys for deeds they hadn't even done yet. Making an assault on La Mort was nerve-racking enough. Athos and Porthos didn't need to know they were going up against an immortal sorcerer as well. Their confidence in their abilities was a strength that Greg and Aramis couldn't afford to undermine.

Greg checked his watch. It was time.

He looked past Aramis, to where Athos and Porthos stood on the riverbank. "Now or never," he said.

"Wait!" Porthos called. He hurried to the water's edge. "I've been thinking . . ."

"That's a first," Athos muttered.

Greg laughed in spite of himself. So did Aramis.

Porthos snickered as well. "Maybe so. I know we've had

our differences, but listen. We're a team now, right? We all have one another's back."

Aramis glanced at Athos sheepishly, as though embarrassed. "Yes, that's right."

"Then it seems we should have an oath of some sort," Porthos went on. "A bond we swear to one another, to seal our friendship. We often use them in the nobility. I remember one time in the Loire Valley—"

"Great idea." Greg cut Porthos off before he could launch into a long story that would delay the whole attack. "How about this? All for one and one for all."

The boys unanimously broke into smiles.

"That's perfect," Athos said. "I really like the sound of that."

I thought you might, Greg answered silently. He stuck out his hand. The other boys all placed theirs on top of it.

"All for one and one for all," they echoed.

Greg stepped into the river and started swimming.

Michel Dinicoeur paced the ramparts of La Mort, inspecting its defenses. Everything he saw confirmed what he'd believed all along: These boys were fools.

Attempting a prison rescue was a suicide mission. The Musketeers he knew—the ones who had thwarted him so long ago—had been different. They were older, wiser, cautious men. They wouldn't have risked their lives for a lost cause. But *these* Musketeers were young, impetuous, and overconfident. They were *teenagers*.

Ever since Dominic Richelieu had informed his future self that the boys were already in league with Greg Rich, Dinicoeur had foreseen everything they'd done. It was a joy consorting with his younger self . . . the incarnation who knew nothing of what could be in store for eternity. Hopefully only great things. And they thought alike, naturally: Both had predicted the boys would attack La Mort. Dinicoeur just hadn't expected the boys would be so moronic about it. No matter. Their escape at Porthos's home last night now seemed like a trivial inconvenience. Thanks to the duplicitous girl, Milady, they'd sealed their own fate. They'd been fool enough to trust her with the time they would attack. And she'd gone straight to Dinicoeur with the information.

So now, all he had to do was have his soldiers prepped and ready at midnight. He smiled down the parapet at the surprise he'd prepared for the Musketeers in the northern turret: a cannon.

That certainly hadn't been in the plans they'd stolen.

It wasn't a huge gun. But it was big enough to do what was needed. The boys had no choice but to come by boat— and once in range, he'd blast them out of the water. And if, by some miracle, they got past the cannon, his soldiers would be waiting. Forty of them. More than enough to dispatch them to their graves.

Dinicoeur reflexively rubbed his prosthetic hand. He

wondered what would happen once the Musketeers were dead. If he killed them before their future selves cut his hand off, would his old hand return? In truth, he'd probably vanish altogether. He'd have irrevocably altered history. If the Musketeers weren't around, then he'd never be sent to the Bastille, which meant there'd be no need for him to track down the Devil's Stone again and return to the past. . . .

The person he was now would cease to exist. And in truth, he could imagine nothing better. The past four hundred years had been one long nightmare. If he vanished—and those memories vanished with him—so be it. What mattered was that Dominic Richelieu would thrive without the Musketeers to thwart him. And even though he, Dinicoeur, *was* Dominic, he didn't feel it. Too much time had passed . . . too many drawn-out, torturous decades. He didn't even think of himself as Dominic anymore. He thought of himself as Michel. But deep in his heart, he knew that Michel was just a facade, a means to an end. Dominic was the one who mattered.

Of course, Dominic had been shocked when Michel had first presented himself. But he'd listened to Michel's story and quickly grasped what needed to be done. He'd disappeared when Michel needed him to—so that none of the soldiers would realize there were two of them—and taken command when he needed to be two places at once. He'd even been proactive at times; when he'd found Greg in the king's quarters with three boys who looked like teen-age versions of the Musketeers Michel had described, he'd acted swiftly and tried to capture them.

Now, Dominic had disappeared into the country-side again, allowing Michel to be the one who took care of the boys once and for all. Dominic understood his older self had dreamed of this moment for centuries. He would let his alter ego have his glory. And then, once the Musketeers—and perhaps Dinicoeur—were gone, he'd be free to track down the Devil's Stone again. In fact, it wouldn't take him long. Michel had told him where it was; after all, he'd found it before. Dominic had already put his plans in motion to get it. Soon he would obtain immortality . . . and amass his riches with impunity.

A delicious thought flickered though Michel's mind. If the trajectory of his life changed, so might that of history. If he remained powerful, the entire future of France and perhaps the world might turn out very differently indeed. The people affected most would be his descendants. Perhaps Stefan would stay by his side rather than flee to America. And if that happened, then Stefan's American descendants—like Gregory and his doltish parents—would never exist either.

And the world would be a much better place.

Michel laughed at the thought. It was a shame he wouldn't be around to see the future he'd create. But this was the only way to give his younger self the life he wanted.

The life he should have had all along. It was hard to believe that everything he'd plotted and planned over nearly four hundred years was finally coming to fruition. At last, after all that time, he would have his revenge.

Tonight, the Musketeers would die.

Aramis thundered toward Paris. The horse Porthos had lent him kicked up dirt with its fierce gallop. The night wind whipped through his hair. His eyes smarted. He kept them pinned on the city lights ahead. He knew why he'd been picked for this solitary part of the mission: because he was the weakest swordsman. Well, perhaps he was better than Greg, though the boy from the future had shown some facility with a blade . . . *fencing*, he'd called it in English.

But Greg was the only one who could swim.

Three boys against a heavily fortified prison. Aramis was secretly relieved not to be in on the attack—though his relief was tempered by guilt that he wasn't involved. Then again, his role wasn't devoid of risk. In fact, it promised to be quite dangerous . . . but he reminded himself of what Greg had confided in him the night before: Focus on the positives.

Rather than pass through the Bastille gate, Aramis circled the city, passing fields of wheat and slowly churning windmills, until he arrived at the main gate by the palace.

Although Aramis was a wanted man, he knew that Richelieu (or Dinicoeur, or perhaps both) had shifted his attention to La Mort for the night. He was expecting the boys to be *there*, not entering the city. As such, his best soldiers would make their stand at the prison. Just as Aramis suspected, the soldiers on guard at the gate were raw and even younger than he was. Alone at night, he didn't look like a threat. They let him pass.

After tying his horse to a tree, Aramis approached the palace. The soldiers posted were similarly young and inexperienced. Several were asleep on the steps. Aramis skulked past them, then clambered up the scaffolding to the second floor and crept along it until he came to the prearranged window.

His heart thumping, he pressed lightly on the window. With a quiet creak, it swung open. Holding his breath, Aramis slipped into the darkness of King Louis's bedroom. A *whoosh* suddenly filled his ears. Aramis caught the gleam of a blade in the moonlight. The tip of it jabbed him in the chest, just to the left of his breastbone, situated perfectly to stab him through the heart.

"Take one more step and you die," the swordsman said.

Athos and Porthos crept along the riverbank, towing the rowboat behind them.

Porthos had bartered with a fisherman earlier that afternoon, trading one of his rings for the boat. The ring was probably worth a hundred times more than the flimsy craft, but Porthos had left his change purse behind when fleeing the estate. Besides, his family owned hundreds of other rings just like it. He could always replace it . . . assuming his father didn't disown him after he'd brought the king's guard to their door.

Porthos had been in trouble before: plenty of times, in fact. But even *he* had the good sense to know that he'd never been in quite as much trouble as this. He figured the saving grace was that this time, he was doing something worthwhile. For the first time in his life, he felt motivated by a noble cause. He wasn't merely having fun. He had no idea if his father would understand—he most likely wouldn't—but Porthos knew he could gladly suffer whatever punishment lay in store . . . if they survived, of course.

The going was slow along the bank. The boat kept getting hung up in reeds and tree roots, and the footing was squishy. Finally they arrived at a preselected tree stump: a perfect jettison point. La Mort loomed in the darkness on its island downstream. Porthos assessed the current of the river. If they put in here and rowed slowly, they'd end up right at the front gate of the prison.

"Do you see him?" Porthos asked.

Athos shook his head, concerned. "I don't."

"Relax. He said he could swim."

"Perhaps he lied. I'm a great athlete and *I* can't swim. Many men far more fit than D'Artagnan would drown en route."

"Well, *he* didn't." Porthos pointed. "Look there!"

Athos peered into the night. Something bobbed in the water not far upstream from the island. The satchel! And then Greg surfaced beside it, just long enough to take a gulp of air before submerging again.

"He's almost there." Porthos pulled the rope hand over hand, reeling in the rowboat. "Time for us to go."

"Silence from here on out," Athos cautioned. "Voices carry across the water."

Porthos stepped into the boat, sat in the gunwale, and seized the oars. It was his job to row, because they needed to save Athos's strength for battle. Athos climbed in, tightly clutching the swords, and pushed the boat away from the bank. Porthos began to paddle toward the deadliest place in France.

The swim was harder than Greg had expected. Growing up in Connecticut, he'd swum in rivers plenty of times, but never at night. And certainly not fully clothed. He'd opted for some stockings and a thin shirt, but even those dragged him down. By the time he felt the ground under his feet, he was exhausted.

He eased out of the river as quietly as possible. Thankfully, La Mort was upstream from Paris; Greg felt he'd swallowed at least a gallon of water during his swim. If he'd been downstream, he'd probably have been poisoned. Plus, he'd stink so badly the guards would be able to smell him.

There was only a small bit of land, perhaps five or six feet across, between the base of the prison wall and the river. Greg was soaking wet, and the breeze made him shiver. There hadn't been room for a towel in his bag . . . not that towels even existed yet. The best he could do was a small rag, which he used to dry his face, hands, and feet. He slipped his shoes on and checked his matches.

His throat caught. Water had leaked into the satchel. His fingers shaking, he tore open the oilskin. If the matches were ruined, the rescue wouldn't work—and he had no way of calling off the others. They'd have already put their plans in motion. To his relief, however, three of the matches were still bone dry. Greg carefully tucked them back in the dry part of the satchel and faced the prison.

The wall was hewn from rough stone, allowing for many hand- and footholds. That was the plus side. In the darkness, of course, it was hard to make them out. When you were fifty feet up, you didn't want to reach for what you *presumed* was a handhold and find out it was only a shadow. Still, there was nowhere to go but up. Greg blew into his hands to warm them, flexed his fingers, and then found his first grip on the stone.

To his surprise, there were gaps between some of the rocks. They were all very narrow, not more than an inch or two, which had made them invisible from the riverbank. With a shudder, he realized they were windows. In drawings Greg had seen of old prisons, there had been much larger spaces to let in light, with iron bars to restrain the prisoners. These slits would allow only a small bit of fresh air and the tiniest sliver of light within each dark and fetid cell.

Greg could hear some of the prisoners as he climbed higher. Ghostlike moans floated on the wind . . . along with what sounded like gibberish. Was it someone talking to himself? Who else did he have to speak to? At least Greg's parents had each other . . . *if* they were even in the same cell.

The slits did have one advantage: They made the climb much easier. Each was a solid foot- or handhold, and with them, Greg made it up the stone face with surprising speed. But he was worn out from the swim. His muscles burned. His legs were starting to spasm—the up-and-down stutter climbers called "sewing machine leg." If he didn't reach the top soon, he would be in trouble. He chanced a look up and saw that the edge of the parapet was only a few feet away. Another five moves and he'd be there. . . .

That was when he heard the footsteps.

Greg clung to the wall tightly and flattened his body against it. Within seconds, his muscles began trembling. His fingers started to slip off the stones. And his right foot was on a lousy hold, a small shard of wobbly stone. He needed to move, but it was impossible to do that without making a noise. And on this silent night, any noise, no matter how soft—a scrape of his leg against the wall, a sharp intake of breath—would alert whoever was patrolling the parapet that he was directly below.

I hate time travel, he thought.

"Monsieur Richelieu, there's a boat approaching."

Dinicoeur took a moment to respond. After so many years, he'd gotten so used to *not* being Richelieu that he sometimes didn't react right away when someone addressed him by his real name. He found a guard standing by his side. "What type of boat?"

"Only a small fishing boat. But you said to be on the lookout for *anything*." The guard pointed across the water, toward the north bank of the river.

Dinicoeur removed a spyglass from his coat and peered through it.

Two figures in a rowboat. Most likely fishermen going after eels. Nothing to worry about. After all, he was expecting four boys. . . . But one of these was rowing hard—toward the prison. Fishermen usually anchored or drifted with the current. He squinted through the lens and twisted the spyglass into focus. In the dim light, he could make out Athos in the bow. He stole a glance at his watch, tucked under the sleeve of his billowy shirt. He'd brought it from the future, as Greg had—but until this moment he'd kept it hidden so as to not raise eyebrows.

It was only nine o'clock.

Dinicoeur gritted his teeth. Rage surged through his veins. The Musketeers had tricked him! Somehow, they had figured out he was in league with Milady. They'd used that against him, giving her a false time for their attack on La Mort. The extra soldiers he'd arranged for weren't here yet. He'd told them to take their places on the riverbank at eleven. Two hours away.

He cursed under his breath. So, he'd underestimated their intelligence. No matter. Perhaps he didn't have all forty men, but he still stood atop an impenetrable fortress—and they were mere *boys*. He didn't know where the other two were, but he had Athos and Porthos, the most able of the bunch, in his sights.

"Prepare the cannon," he ordered.

"I mean no harm," Aramis whispered in the vast darkness of the king's bedchamber, the sword still pressed tightly to his chest.

"And yet, you have snuck into my home in the middle of the night."

Aramis blinked, recognizing the voice. "King Louis?"

"Who were you expecting to find in my room at this hour?"

"You, of course, Your Majesty. It's just that . . . I thought you'd be asleep. Not armed with a sword. I'm a friend."

The king sniffed. "My friends usually enter through the front door."

"I mean, I met you here the other day. In this very room. I was with three other boys." Aramis swallowed hard. He feared at any second he'd misspeak and the king would stab him right through the heart. "We have learned of something that is a great threat to you, and I needed to tell you of it immediately."

"Then why didn't you tell my guards? They are charged with my protection."

"Because I couldn't trust any of them, Your Highness."

There was silence. Finally, Aramis felt the sword pressed against his chest relax slightly. "I understand it was Milady de Winter who led you here yesterday," the king said. "She claims you all infiltrated the queen's quarters."

"True, Your Highness." It took every ounce of self-control Aramis possessed not to move suddenly. "We did not intend to trespass. It was an accident. But that's indeed where we met Milady. She's very concerned for your safety. She's the one who unlocked your window this evening, so that I might come to you."

The king was silent again. "What were they like?" he murmured.

Aramis blinked in the darkness. "I beg your forgiveness. What was what like?"

"The queen's quarters. I've never seen them." Louis's tone seemed to soften a little. "Unlike some people, I'm not free to roam about, breaking into any rooms I wish."

"Oh, well . . . They were very nice. Very tasteful. The queen will be pleased with them, I think." Aramis was surprised. The line of questioning didn't seem very regal. But then he had to remind himself: The king was only fourteen, even younger than he was.

"That's good to hear." Louis lowered his sword from Aramis's chest and sheathed it. "Now tell me about this trouble I'm in."

"I'm afraid there's not enough time to explain it all here," Aramis said. "I don't suppose you'd care to go for a ride?"

As Greg listened to Dinicoeur above, the wobbly stone beneath his right foot gave way. The night seemed to spin around him. His right leg dangled over the void. The fingers on his right hand slipped free. . . . But somehow, his left hand maintained its grip. He smacked into the stone wall, letting out a groan. The rock that had come loose tumbled away. After a long drop, it plopped into the Seine.

Above, Greg spotted a pair of gloved hands grip the edge of the wall.

He scrambled for another foothold. It didn't matter how much noise he made now. Once a guard saw him, he'd have to move—

A blinding explosion nearly tossed him off the wall. He cringed, feeling the concussion tremble through the entire prison. The quake was followed instantly by the screaming whistle of a cannonball. His eyes widened in horror as a geyser of water burst from where it struck the river.

La Mort has a cannon? he thought, panicked. *No. That wasn't in the plans.*

The gloved fingers withdrew from the wall above, and booted footsteps raced toward the sounds of the explosion. Greg heaved a sigh of relief. Funny: The cannon had saved his life. Not so funny: It very well might kill Porthos and Athos. But the guard had left his post. Greg leaped into action. He found a foothold, then a handhold, then a few more. Within seconds, he had reached the top of the wall.

Every guard had abandoned his post and raced to the far corner, where the cannon sat on a turret. Thankfully it must have missed its target, because they were all lining up their muskets and firing into the night. So, Athos and Porthos had diverted the attention of Dinicoeur's men, but it wouldn't be long before a musket ball—or worse, another cannonball—found them. Greg's limbs felt like lead, but there was no time to rest. He rolled over the top of the wall and dropped onto the parapet.

The prison was laid out exactly how Porthos had described—save for the cannon. Greg raced around the parapet toward the turret on the opposite corner. The guards were so focused on the river that no one even glanced his way. Within seconds, he was scurrying down a spiral staircase and into La Mort's interior.

The building shook as the cannon fired once more. The dark stairwell echoed with shouts, screams, and agonized howls. Clearly, the prisoners had no idea what was going on. To Greg, it felt as if he were descending into some nightmare version of the afterlife. It was so dark he didn't realize he'd reached the very bottom until he stumbled on the rough stone floor.

He found himself in a large room lit only by two oil lamps hung high on the walls. The massive oak doors of the prison stood before him. A smaller alcove sat to the left. There was no door on it. What would be the point of locking something *inside* an impenetrable fortress? There, as Porthos had promised, was the armory. A dozen muskets lined the walls, along with crossbows and swords. Below them was a low-slung bench, on which rested crates of musket balls and gunpowder cartridges.

Then Greg spied something even better: a huge barrel of gunpowder. Greg shoved it onto its side, pulled the plug, and rolled it to the doors, leaving a thick black trail. Then he tossed all the weapons on top of it—except for one sword and one musket, which he kept for himself. Though he hadn't been the least bit quiet, the sound was swallowed up by the screams of the prisoners and the gunfire above.

Greg retreated to the safety of the alcove and struck the first match.

It flared quickly and vanished just as fast. A dud. There were only two left. His fingers shook again. He took out the second, set it against the matchbook, and—

"What do you think you're doing?"

Greg looked up, startled.

A guard stood before him, aiming a musket his way.

"That's a cannon!" Athos yelled.

"I know!" Porthos yelled back, struggling to keep the rocking boat from tipping over from the waves the cannonball had kicked up. "I can see it!"

"You didn't say anything about a cannon!"

"Of course I didn't!" Porthos barked. "It wasn't there before!"

Getting spotted had been part of the plan. D'Artagnan would never have been able to reach the armory unless they could distract the guards. They'd even expected the muskets. But muskets were inaccurate. And unless they were loaded perfectly, which they rarely were, they tended not to shoot very far. A cannon, however, was a whole different story.

"How far can a cannonball travel?" Athos asked.

A column of water exploded only five feet to their right, drenching them and filling the boat with startled fish.

"Apparently this far," Porthos replied.

"Then back up!" Athos hissed as the boat swayed violently again. He crouched low, gripping the sides tightly. "Get out of range!"

"What do you think I'm trying to do?" Porthos pulled hard on the oars, only to find one had been splintered in half. "The problem is, if we get too far away, we'll be swept downstream. And . . ." He didn't have to finish. Athos knew what he was thinking. Greg would be stranded in La

Mort with a dozen soldiers.

Athos had bravely faced many things in his life. But this time, he had to admit he was scared. If a cannonball hit their boat, it would either kill them immediately or plunge them into the river. Either way, they were dead. *Please, D'Artagnan*, he thought. *We need you to come through for us. Where are you?*

Greg lifted his hands over his head, but kept them together, concealing the match and the matchbook.

"What's in your hands?" the guard demanded.

Greg realized his opponent wasn't much older than he was. And he seemed just as shaken by all the commotion. Working in a place like this probably took a toll on you.

"It's nothing," Greg said. "Just a little piece of wood. See?"

He snapped the match against the matchbook. It flared to life. He had only one advantage over the armed guard. He'd seen a match before.

The guard stepped back, terrified, his eyes locked on the flame. "Are—are you a sorcerer?" he stammered.

Greg didn't answer. He simply dropped the match and dove inside the alcove. The gunpowder flared as the match hit it. The fire raced along the dark trail, straight toward the barrel. . . . Greg squeezed his eyes shut and clamped his hands over his ears.

KA-BOOOOM!

The massive explosion rattled Greg's bones and sent him

rolling across the floor. The entire building shook. For a panicked moment, he thought it might collapse.

His ears ringing, Greg crawled from the alcove and found the prison a very different place than it had been seconds before. Every surface was scorched black, with fires burning everywhere. The huge oak doors had been blown off their hinges and sailed into the river. The weapons he'd piled atop the gunpowder keg were ruined, either lying in charred pieces or embedded in the stone walls. The guard lay sprawled on the floor, having been tossed several feet across the room. His arms and legs were bleeding, but he was alive. His gun was nowhere to be seen.

Greg placed his sword against the guard's neck. "There's a man and a woman here, due to be hung tomorrow. Where are they?"

The young guard was too shaken to respond. He could only point down the hall.

That was all Greg needed. The rest of the guards were coming. He could hear them thundering down the stairs. He took one gunpowder cartridge and then threw the rest of the crate onto the fire. Then he grabbed a flaming piece of wood to use as a torch and set off to find his parents.

TWENTY-THREE

"HE DID IT!" ATHOS STARED AT THE FLAMING GAP WHERE the prison doors had been blown clear. Despite the cannon and the muskets and the rocking boat, the sight filled him with courage. "Let's row!"

"But what about the—," Porthos began.

Athos pointed to the parapets. The other guards were abandoning their posts to race to the site of the explosion. "Forget about the cannon. They have."

Porthos handed Athos the shattered oar. "Very well. But I could use a little help."

"Mom! Dad! Where are you?" Greg raced through the maze of passages, clutching the architectural plans of La Mort and his sword in one hand and the makeshift torch in the other, with the musket slung over his shoulder. His route was descending, carved into the island. The builders had lined the earth with stone to keep the river at bay, but with the explosion, the foundation had started to fail. Liquid oozed through the cracks and there were puddles everywhere. The whole place smelled of mold and damp and rot.

In the distance behind him, Greg heard a series of small explosions. That would have been the crate of cartridges he'd dumped onto the fire. The wood had burned through and now the cartridges were going off. Hopefully, it would provide enough cover to slow down the guards for a bit.

A bigger explosion followed. Probably the cannon again, though perhaps something else in the armory had blown up. The entire building shook once more. Dust rained from the ceiling above. A frightening thought came to Greg: If La Mort had been built by less-than-talented masons, how sturdy was it?

He was beginning to lose hope. He'd only been going for a few minutes, but the prison wasn't *that* big. It seemed he should have located his parents by now. Perhaps the guard had pointed to the wrong passage. Or perhaps Greg had misread the plans and made a wrong turn. Or maybe they were already dead. Dinicoeur didn't need them alive to lure Greg over here. . . .

"Greg?" The voice sounded like a croak.

"Mom! Where are you?"

"Greg!" his dad groaned. "This way!"

Greg froze and shut his eyes, listening as hard as he could. They called his name again, but it echoed wildly among the other shouts and explosions. He dashed forward to a fork in the passageway. "Mom? Dad?" he shouted.

"This way!" This time, the voices came from the left.

"Keep calling as loud as you can!" Greg instructed, following the sound. The fact that his parents spoke English made it easier to pick them out among the other anguished pleas and cries. The passageway plunged even deeper, down a slick flight of stairs, burrowing into the damp earth. Even with the torch, Greg could barely see a foot in front of his face.

"Mom? Dad? Keep calling—"

"We're here!"

Greg stopped. The voices were almost right next to him. He turned and squinted at a wooden door only four feet high, rotting from the dampness. He thumped on it—and heard cries of joy from the other side. "That's us!" Dad shouted, his voice clear and strong now, only slightly muffled. "Help!"

"Stand back!" Greg drove his foot into the door. Despite

the rot, it was sturdily locked in place, and he didn't have a key.

"What's happening?" his mother cried.

"Relax, Mom. I'm getting you out of here." Greg hoped he sounded reassuring, because he had only one idea left. If it didn't work, he didn't know what to do. He jammed the gunpowder cartridge he'd taken into the keyhole, touched the torch to the linen casing, and then dove for cover. "Get down and cover your heads—"

A loud *bang* silenced him before he could finish. The lock blew out and clanged off the far wall. Greg waved the smoke away and found the door hanging ajar. He shoved it aside . . . and nearly gagged. His parents' eyes, wide open in surprise, reflected the torch. They were the brightest points of light in the cell. It was nothing more than a pit: too far below the surface for there to be a window, with a ceiling so low an adult couldn't stand upright. The floor was a soup of mud.

His parents piled on him, hugging him, clinging to him tightly, as though to prove to themselves that he was really there. Both wept, overwhelmed by joy. "Thank goodness you're all right," his father managed. "We thought we'd never see you again."

"We had no idea if you were even alive," his mother cried.

"I'm fine," Greg managed shakily. "Though I'll be a whole lot better once we're out of here. Come on!" He led them back the way he'd come. He could tell his parents had a thousand questions, but they understood the urgency. Neither spoke as they raced after him—stooped and filthy, their bare feet caked with mud.

Greg thought he remembered the way back to the entrance, but with all the echoing chaos, he grew confused. Eventually, they came upon a hallway filled with smoke, which seemed promising. But it was also disorienting, as it was now almost impossible for Greg to see where he was going. He coughed and squinted, creeping toward the flames. He and his parents had to stoop so low to stay under the smoke they were practically crawling, until, to Greg's incredible relief, he spotted the entrance ahead.

The fire was blazing uncontrollably now. Many of the guards were trying to fight it, dragging buckets of water from the river and throwing them at the blaze. Others seemed unsure what to do at all. In the smoke and the confusion, Greg chanced a run straight through the entry hall to the arch where the doors had once been—

Only to find Valois blocking his path. The burly captain stood in the exit, his piggish eyes and sword gleaming in the firelight. Greg couldn't believe it. To have come so far, to have nearly saved his parents . . . only to be killed here now?

"You're not going anywhere," Valois snarled.

An oar swung out of the darkness behind him, thwacking him on the head hard enough to knock him off his feet.

He face-planted on the stone, unconscious.

Athos and Porthos leaped through the arch. "Sorry we're late," Porthos said cheerfully.

Four guards dropped their buckets and went for their swords, but Athos was ready. He kicked a pile of flaming embers into their faces, temporarily blinding them, then deftly proceeded to disarm all four—sending their swords skidding into the flames.

Another pair of guards attacked from the other side, but Porthos charged with the oar, driving both men into a wall.

"Get your parents to the boat!" he shouted at Greg.

Greg was already one step ahead of him, dragging his parents outside to the small prison dock. Four boats had been tied up there, but Porthos and Athos had cut all but one free. They were now drifting toward Paris, along with the rowboat. Only one vessel remained: the one that had carried the cannon to the prison.

As Greg herded his parents to it, he heard footsteps racing toward him. He spun around to find a guard charging him, blade extended. Before he even knew what he was doing, Greg whipped out the sword he'd swiped from the armory and deflected the strike.

With a strange detachment, Greg realized: *This is my very first swordfight.*

It was different from fencing—this sword was a lot heavier, for one thing—but there were enough similarities that Greg was able to handle himself. He held his breath, adrenaline coursing through him. They parried time and again, dancing around the dock, switching from offense to defense and back. Greg caught a glimpse of Athos, dispatching an onslaught of attacking guards with ease. Athos bounced one's head off the stairs, speared another through his shirt and pinned him to the wall, then managed to set the next one's pants on fire—sending him screaming into the water.

Greg was nowhere near as adept as Athos. Furthermore, the swim, the climb, and the rescue had been exhausting. He was cruising on fumes now, fighting to lift the blade each time. His opponent seemed to be gaining strength, sensing that Greg was weakening. He went on the offensive, hacking so hard at Greg's sword that sparks flew. Greg backed onto a wobbly plank. It shifted under his weight. He lost his balance and crashed to the dock.

The guard raised his sword, ready to plunge it through Greg's chest—when a coil of rope suddenly whipped over his head.

Behind him, Greg's parents yanked on both ends. The rope snapped tight across the guard's chest, flinging him backward into the river. Greg didn't have time to thank them, however. Porthos and Athos were charging out of the prison at full speed.

"Untie the boat!" Porthos yelled. "He's coming!"

Sure enough, Dinicoeur emerged from the building behind them. The madman was so consumed by rage, so intent on vengeance, that he no longer looked human. Backlit by the flames, he looked positively satanic.

Greg's parents untied the boat and shoved it away from the dock. Porthos leaped in. Athos was almost there. . . . Suddenly Greg noticed something in Dinicoeur's prosthetic hand: a small black ball with a flaming wick.

"Athos!" Greg shouted. "He's got a bomb!"

Athos whirled around at the same moment that Dinicoeur raised his hand to throw the bomb. In the blink of an eye, Athos threw his sword. It spun through the air— and severed Dinicoeur's fake hand from his arm.

For a moment, Dinicoeur seemed more startled than hurt. As if he couldn't believe—after all these years, after all his plotting, after centuries of nothing but obsessing over revenge—that Athos had done the same thing to him *again*.

And then Dinicoeur visibly realized the more pressing problem. His hand—and the bomb—had tumbled back toward the prison. The explosion tossed Dinicoeur through the air like a scrap of paper. The already weakened front arch of the prison crumbled and collapsed.

The explosion caught Athos in midair as he leaped from the dock. He tumbled into the boat and nearly flew off the other side, but Greg caught him and held him tight.

Somewhere in the darkness, there was a splash as Dinicoeur landed in the Seine.

Porthos dug the oars into the water. The current caught

the boat and quickly pulled it downstream. Guards scrambled over the toppled prison wall, only to find there were no boats left at the dock. They were trapped on the island.

"I'd say that went quite well," Porthos croaked, his lungs heaving. He flashed an impish smile, the flames dancing in his eyes.

"I could have done without all the people trying to kill us," Greg muttered.

He glanced at his parents. They were filthy and frail-looking after only three days. They smelled of mold and sweat—and their haunted eyes bulged from their gaunt faces, still in shock at all they had seen. But they were alive. The other boys gallantly took the oars and allowed Greg to sit between his parents. He was almost able to relax as they pulled ashore.

Where Dominic Richelieu and the king's guard stood waiting for them.

TWENTY-FOUR

Forty soldiers armed with muskets swept toward the boat as the boys and Greg's parents clambered onto dry land. There was no point in trying to escape. There would be no getting past them. Richelieu appeared in the middle of their ranks, perched atop a black horse. Greg knew it was the younger man: He wore no gloves, revealing two hands of flesh and blood. Besides, Dinicoeur had been blown into the river.

"These people are criminals, all guilty of treason against the Crown," he shouted at the troops. "Fire at will!"

"You will do no such thing!" The voice rang out through the night.

The eyes of each soldier went wide at the sound of it, though no one was more surprised than Richelieu. He spun around to see two more figures on horseback emerge from the night. Aramis . . . and King Louis XIII.

Greg turned to his parents. Their jaws hung wide. But for the first time that night, he saw a twinkle in their fatigued eyes.

"No one shall be condemned to death unless by the order of the king," Louis stated, tugging on his reins and pulling his horse up short. "That is the law, is it not?"

"Of course, Your Majesty." Richelieu bowed respectfully from his horse. "I apologize if I overstepped my bounds, but I did so only for your protection. These people have committed treason. And for that, the penalty is death."

"Then I'd worry about my own neck if I were you," Athos said. "You've committed far worse treason than any of us."

Richelieu snorted. "You have just laid siege to a royal prison! I have done nothing but serve my king!"

"So . . . he knows about the letter you sent Milady de Winter off with last night?" Porthos asked.

Richelieu gasped in astonishment. "I did no such thing."

"Oh, no?" Greg demanded. "Because I *saw* you do it. And then I followed Milady to Saint-Germain-des-Prés. I'm sure either she or the monks there would reveal the truth if His Majesty the king asked them. Or perhaps the envoy from another country she met at the inn could help us—"

"All right!" Richelieu shouted. "I sent out a letter!"

"Then why was I not told of it?" Louis demanded. Greg was impressed; the boy's voice was full of calm authority, unlike how he'd sounded back at the palace.

"It didn't seem worth troubling you over, Your Highness." Richelieu forced a fake smile. "It was just an unimportant missive."

"Sent out under the cover of night?" Louis asked. "And delivered by a handmaiden? It appears you've been doing quite a lot behind my back lately."

"If I have offended you, I beg your forgiveness once again," Richelieu said. "I have done nothing but serve my king and France, while these boys have destroyed a prison to free two people who planned to assassinate you!"

"Indeed. My friend Aramis here says these prisoners were condemned to death for their acts. Is that true?" Louis asked.

"That's correct," Richelieu replied.

"I don't recall issuing that decree, either," Louis snapped. "Did you?"

"Er, yes, but . . . ," Richelieu stammered. "But it was in your best interests! They infiltrated the palace three nights ago with intent to kill you!"

Louis fixed Richelieu with a harsh stare. "So you say. Although I've noticed that what you say isn't always the truth."

"This time it is, sire," Richelieu mewled. "I assure you."

"Well, I suppose we could investigate that," the king said. "And while we're at it, we might want to talk to some of the other prisoners in La Mort and see if they really did what they're in there for . . . or if they've only been put away because you ordered it."

Richelieu swallowed hard. "Why would you say that, Your Majesty?"

"Aramis and I had a very enlightening discussion on the way here," Louis said. "It seems many of the prisoners in that jail are there only because you sent them there."

"It is true, I have sentenced some," Richelieu admitted. "But never an innocent party. Everyone I've condemned has been guilty!" His voice rose, as if he were forgetting himself. "I have the authority, do I not, to mete out punishment? If I have the intelligence to perceive someone is a criminal, then shouldn't I, as a member of the government, be able to mete out punishment?"

"So by that logic," said Louis, "I should be able to do the same?"

"Of course, Your Majesty," Richelieu replied.

Louis turned to the soldiers. "Take Monsieur Richelieu prisoner at once. I perceive he is a criminal."

The soldiers seemed surprised, but none hesitated. They'd probably never received a direct order from the king himself. They turned their muskets on Richelieu, who went white with shock.

"Your Majesty! You can't do this!"

"I can do anything I want." Louis smiled. "I'm the king, remember?"

The soldiers quickly closed in on Richelieu. "Where should we take him, sire?" asked a captain.

Louis looked across the river to where La Mort was still burning. "I'm afraid La Mort is no longer an option. I believe there's a dungeon in the Bastille. Lock him up there. That should require only a few men. The rest of you, take some boats out to the island, put out that fire, and attend to the prisoners."

"And what are we to do about these boys?" the captain asked.

Louis studied the four boys one by one: Greg, Athos, Porthos, and Aramis. "I'll keep an eye on them."

"Sire? I must protest—," the captain began.

"I'll be all right," Louis said. "Now get that fire out. That's an order."

The soldiers scurried off. Once they were gone, Aramis turned to Louis. "Thank you, Your Majesty. . . ."

"No, I should be thanking *you*. This has been a fascinating night." Louis looked up at the stars. "Is it always this beautiful out here?"

"Well, there are usually fewer prison fires, Your Highness," Porthos said. "But otherwise, yes."

"I'd forgotten." Louis sighed. "I haven't been outside the palace alone at night since . . . Well, I can't remember. Since before my father was killed, I'll bet. Richelieu has always insisted I stay inside for my safety. But it seems there are many ways of making someone a prisoner." Louis turned to Greg and his parents. "So, you're all deadly assassins, are you?"

Greg's parents knelt reverently. "No, My Lord," said Dad.

"I think he was being sarcastic," Greg whispered.

"Your Majesty." Athos stepped forward. "While you're putting criminals away, there's another you should know about. Richelieu's twin brother. Last we saw him, he was out in the river somewhere."

"Oh?" Louis scanned the choppy water and shrugged.

"You don't seem very surprised about that," Greg said.

"Aramis told me about him as well," Louis replied. "Like I said, it's been fascinating. I knew people were plotting against me, but I never suspected it was the head of my own guard and his evil twin. And if his twin is still alive, he probably won't last long. Not in that water, and not with my soldiers combing the riverbanks. I suppose, with both gone, I'll probably need someone else in charge of security."

"I'd say so," Porthos agreed. "Someone trustworthy this time."

Louis regarded the four boys and smiled. "I don't suppose you'd all be interested?"

In the woods nearby, Milady de Winter watched the king and the boys from atop her horse. She was too far away to clearly hear all that was said, but she could tell what had happened. Richelieu had been revealed as a traitor and taken prisoner.

Milady smiled. Everything had worked out so much better than she could have possibly hoped. For months, she'd been looking for a way to unseat Richelieu. Now these peculiar boys had come along and played right into her hands. With Richelieu out of the way, she was now free to enact the plans she'd devised long ago. She snapped on the reins, ready to ride. . . .

But a few words from the king drifted to her through the night. Milady reined in her horse before it could go far. Had she heard correctly? Had the king just asked the boys to be his private security force? Interesting . . . and a surprise.

Although not one she couldn't handle. Milady knew Athos was suspicious of her . . . while Aramis trusted her wholeheartedly. She could use both their feelings to her advantage. After all, they were just *boys*.

It wouldn't be hard to manipulate them.

It fact, it might even be fun.

Milady laughed to herself, then spurred her horse and galloped away.

LE FIN

ONE WEEK
LATER . . .

TWENTY-FIVE

"D'Artagnan! You have to see this!" Aramis whispered.

Greg turned to his friend, surprised. "Now? The ceremony's about to begin!"

"It's important," Aramis hissed.

Greg glanced anxiously around the room where everything had begun: the room in the Louvre where he and his parents had tumbled out of the future and into the past. Only this time, he'd been invited. This time, he wouldn't flee the building with the king's security chasing him. This time, *he* was the king's security.

Only the other boys and their immediate families were present, along with King Louis and a few servants. Louis had proven to be a surprisingly normal teenager on the night of the prison break, but today, to make the right impression on all the families, he was in an exceptionally formal mode. He was dressed in red velvet robes draped with ermine, and carried a jewel-encrusted scepter the size of a polo mallet. He also wore a ridiculously large white wig . . . even though he'd confessed to Greg that he loathed it because it made his scalp itch.

While everyone's families were thrilled to be invited to the palace, Greg's mother and father were understandably the most stunned. During their horrifying days in La Mort, they had given up hope of survival. Now, they beamed at Greg, as if returning to the future didn't even matter anymore. All that mattered to them was that their family was together again.

Like the other boys, Greg had been provided with a dashing outfit, tailored just for him. It was similar to the uniform of a French soldier, only with a wide-brimmed black hat and a blue jacket inlaid with a large fleur-de-lis. "We must face facts," Porthos had remarked earlier, while the boys had stood together before one of the king's massive mirrors. "We look terribly handsome in these."

"Athos, Aramis, Porthos, and D'Artagnan, please approach the throne!" ordered the king.

The boys dutifully lined up shoulder to shoulder and

began to cross the room in a slow, stately manner. Even Porthos behaved himself for once. Greg focused on maintaining a stoic countenance as well, but Aramis had piqued his interest.

"What's so important?" Greg whispered to him.

Aramis jerked his head over his shoulder. There, in the doorway, stood Milady de Winter, her long blond hair cascading down her shoulders. She smiled at them. "I told you we could trust her," Aramis said, grinning broadly.

Greg glanced at Athos and found him glowering; he'd spotted Milady as well and wasn't so pleased by her presence. "I suppose we can," Greg told Aramis, though he wasn't quite sure himself.

"Could you girls quit whispering?" Porthos muttered. "What we're doing here is serious."

Greg and Aramis fell silent as they reached the king's throne and knelt before it.

Louis spoke to everyone in the room. "It is no surprise to anyone here that the last several days have been quite eventful. And sadly, we face more danger."

Greg and the other boys knew exactly what he meant. Michel Dinicoeur had escaped. His footprints had been found on the muddy riverbank—but despite scouring the countryside, the army had not found him.

Louis continued, "As recent events have proven that I cannot trust even my closest adviser, I have decided to create a security force that answers only to me: the Musketeers."

He snapped his fingers. Four servants came forward. Each carried a silver sword on a velvet pillow.

Louis took the first and spoke to Athos. "You have been chosen for your exceptional valor and skill in battle. Your abilities may not have been appreciated in the military, but I assure you, they will be here."

Athos graciously took the sword and bowed. "Thank you, Your Majesty."

His parents gasped in awe. Greg noticed that of all the parents, Athos's mother and father were the most humbled by their surroundings. Clearly neither of them had ever dreamed they might someday be invited to the palace. They were dressed in their finest clothes, which were still threadbare.

Louis turned next to Porthos. "I would never have expected you to show such valor, but your bravery and skill have impressed me. Plus, every team needs a member who can adapt and improvise."

For once, Porthos appeared to be at a loss for words. He simply took the sword and bowed.

Louis handed the third sword to Aramis. "You have been chosen for your great intelligence and ingenuity. Every team needs a wise man to lead it. You will make a wonderful captain of the Musketeers."

Aramis, too, bowed without a word. He shot one more glance back at Milady and blushed.

King Louis stood before Greg with the fourth sword.

"And now for you, D'Artagnan, the last Musketeer. I hear you can swim rivers like a fish, climb stone walls like a spider, and conjure flame like a sorcerer. But you also possess a skill far more important. You know how to make friends and win the trust of others. To come to Paris, knowing no one, and then unite such a fine group of young men for a practically impossible mission within only three days, well . . . that is something few people are capable of. No team will work without someone to hold it together. That is your job in the Musketeers."

Surprised by the king's words, Greg turned to look at the other boys.

"Even if you do talk strangely," Porthos cracked.

Aramis elbowed him in the ribs.

They weren't merely fellow Musketeers, Greg realized. It was strange, but even though he'd only known them all for a very short time, he felt closer to them than to any friends he'd ever made. For the first time in his life, Greg felt as though he belonged somewhere—and that *he'd* earned that belonging.

He did want to return to the future some day. No doubt his parents wanted to even more. But to do that, they had to track down the Devil's Stone. And wherever it was, Dinicoeur was out there somewhere looking for it too. Finding it—and defeating Dinicoeur once and for all—wouldn't be easy. But the prospect of being stuck in medieval France (at least for the time being) no longer seemed like a prison sentence. In fact, now that Greg was surrounded by friends . . . it might actually be fun.

Greg graciously accepted the sword from King Louis.

"It is my honor to serve you," he said. "I won't let you down—"

"Your Majesty!" a voice shouted from the back of the room. A soldier burst in, trailed by an embarrassed servant. Greg noticed that Milady had vanished. Upon seeing the ceremony in progress, the soldier knelt and bowed his head. "I greatly regret the interruption, Your Majesty, but there is an emergency. There has been an attack on the Bastille. Dominic Richelieu has escaped."

Greg immediately knew who was responsible. "Dinicoeur."

The other boys nodded agreement. Athos turned to Louis. "Are the formalities taken care of, Your Highness?"

"Yes," the king replied. "You are all fully deputized agents of my authority."

"Then there's no time to waste." Aramis raised his new sword in the air.

Greg and his other friends all did the same, touching the tips together.

"All for one . . . ," Greg began.

". . . and one for all!" the others replied.

Then they sheathed their swords and ran for their horses.

The swashbuckling adventures
of Greg and the Musketeers continue in

The Last Musketeer: Traitor's Chase

ONE

Paris

GREG RICH CREPT SLOWLY THROUGH THE LOUVRE, clutching his sword tightly, fearing an attack at any second. Flickering torches lighted the rough-hewn stone walls as he made his way along the dirt floor. A rat scurried past him, no doubt to its burrow between the gaps in the stone, while clusters of bats hung from the high, shadowed ceiling. Although clad in his Musketeer's uniform—bright blue with the emblem of the king, a white fleur-de-lis, embroidered on it—the chill air made Greg shiver.

He was in the oldest section of the palace, a remnant

from when the Louvre was a fortress on the western edge of Paris. It was hard to believe this was actually part of the home of the king of France.

The bells of Notre Dame chimed in the distance. It was seven o'clock at night, and although back in the twenty-first century, it wouldn't have been late, here in the seventeenth, most people were already turning in for the night. The sound of the bells made Greg uneasy; two months before, he'd nearly been killed by Michel Dinicoeur in that bell tower.

As Greg edged through the dim corridors, he struggled to remain calm, practicing what Athos had taught him: breathe slowly, be alert to everything around you, keep your sword unsheathed so you're always prepared for . . .

Trouble. Bat squeaks and the flutter of wings alerted Greg that someone was approaching from behind. He spun, his sword at the ready, just as his attacker lunged from the dark passage. A blade glinted in the torchlight, clanging against Greg's own.

Greg took a swordsman's stance, right foot forward, and parried. Athos's lessons filtered through his mind. *Stay in the moment. Focus. No matter how hard he tries not to, your attacker will always signal what he's going to do next. Predict, prepare—and counter.*

Greg watched his opponent's hands and feet, guessed where the strikes would come next, and responded. They ducked and dodged, steel hitting steel. Still, Greg was on the defensive, forced to back down the passage as his attacker surged forward. But then, Greg saw his opening. He deflected a slash at his head, twirled to the right, and attacked.

His instincts were dead on. He had a direct shot at the heart. . . .

"Drop it," a voice hissed in his ear. Suddenly, there was another sword at his throat, cold metal biting against his skin.

Greg let his sword clatter to the ground.

"What'd you do that for?" the voice behind him asked, far less sinister this time.

"Uh . . ." Greg said. "Because you told me to."

"Why would you do what the bad guy tells you to?" The sword lowered from Greg's neck, allowing him to face the second attacker: Porthos. "After all, he's the bad guy. He's not looking out for your best interests."

"Well, what was I supposed to do?" Greg asked. "Outduel two men while there's a sword pressed to my neck?"

"Yes." Athos—the first attacker—emerged from the shadows. "If that had been Michel Dinicoeur or Dominic Richelieu behind you, your head would no longer be attached to your body. How do you expect to catch the madmen if you give up so easily?"

"Maybe *you* can beat two men in that situation," Greg said. "But I can't."

"Then I'd recommend not getting into that situation,"

Athos replied coolly. "You should *always* be prepared for an attack from behind. No matter what."

Greg sighed and picked up his sword. Athos was right, of course. Which only reinforced the fact that, even after two months of training, Greg still felt way out of his league in a swordfight.

"Hey"—Athos put a reassuring arm around Greg's shoulders—"you're doing great. Honestly. If it hadn't been for Porthos, you'd have got me right in the chest."

"Yeah. I would have." Greg mustered a smile. "I almost did you in."

"Oh, I wouldn't say *that*." Athos thumped his hand against the metal breastplate over his heart. "This is *me* we're talking about. I still had a few tricks up my sleeve. But virtually anyone else, you would have beaten. You've come a long way in a short time."

Greg appreciated the praise, though he was also daunted by it. Sometimes he forgot this wasn't just for sport, like all those years of fencing lessons had been back in prep school. Now that he was a Musketeer, knowing how to handle a sword could be the difference between life and death. Especially when Michel Dinicoeur and Dominic Richelieu were out there somewhere, plotting against him.

It had been two months since Michel had sprung Dominic from the Bastille. The attack had come mere minutes after Greg and the others had been sworn in as Musketeers by King Louis XIII. Even though the

Bastille was a massive protected fortress, it had proven little challenge for Michel. The guards had claimed Michel had used sorcery, rendering men unconscious with a mere touch and making the walls explode with a single incantation. Once free, both men had ridden north of the city and crossed the Seine—and when the guards had tried to follow, they'd been repelled by a fusillade of arrows, courtesy of René Valois, a staunch supporter of Michel and Dominic who had once been a leader of the King's Guard. By the time the Musketeers arrived on the scene, Michel and Dominic were long gone.

Greg still had no idea where they were, although he assumed they'd gone off to recover the Devil's Stone. Michel needed it to make his younger self, Dominic, immortal—for if Dominic died, then Michel would cease to exist. Greg wanted to find the stone just as badly as they did—perhaps more—for without it, he couldn't return to his own time. But now his enemies had a two-month head start tracking it down—and once they had it, Greg suspected he'd never get it back. He and his parents would be trapped in 1615 France.

Of course, there was always the possibility that Michel and Dominic hadn't gone after the stone at all but were merely lurking about Paris, waiting for the best opportunity to kill Greg and the Musketeers—a scenario Greg found equally unsettling.

Therefore, Greg had spent the past two months doing

one of two things: training with Athos and Porthos—or sleuthing with Aramis, the brains of the Musketeers. Aramis had gone out today to follow up on a lead, but Greg feared that this would end like all the others: nowhere.

"All right," Athos said, brandishing his sword. "Let's try this again, shall we? Porthos and I will set up another ambush. . . ."

"Another?" Porthos groaned. "Haven't we ambushed him enough?"

"Practice makes perfect," Athos replied. "Besides, it's not like we have anything better to do."

"*I* do," Porthos shot back. "A lady friend of mine needs an escort to a ball this evening. And she has some friends who could use escorts as well, if you're interested."

Greg glanced at Athos, thinking that a ball might be a nice change of pace from the endless training, but the young swordsman frowned. "There are deadly enemies on the loose," he said. "We have no time for dancing."

"I'll bet you wouldn't say that if Milady de Winter needed an escort," Porthos replied with a smirk.

Athos flushed red at the mention of Milady, though Greg couldn't tell if it was from embarrassment or anger—or both. "I have no interest in the queen's handmaiden," he snapped.

Before Porthos could reply, footsteps echoed through the passageway. The three boys immediately raised their swords.

A palace messenger boy rounded the corner and shrieked in fright upon seeing the three blades pointed his way.

"Sorry!" Greg said, lowering his sword. "Didn't mean to scare you!"

"It's my fault," the boy apologized. "I'm sorry, sir." He knelt and bowed his head reverentially.

Greg and the others had been getting a lot of this type of respect since becoming Musketeers. Greg found it a little creepy, although the others ate it up. Even Aramis, who felt that pride was a sin.

"What brings you to interrupt our training?" Athos asked the messenger.

"The king requests a presence with D'Artagnan," the boy replied.

After all his time in France, Greg was finally getting used to being called D'Artagnan. His real name was only known to Aramis, one of many secrets he was forced to keep.

"Guess you'd better make haste, then." Athos tried to sound light of heart, although Greg could hear the jealousy beneath it.

"All right." Greg sheathed his sword and followed the messenger down the passage. He could feel the others staring after him, wondering what the king could possibly want with him this time.

The messenger led him from the old fortress into the true palace. The dirt floors became wood, and the stone walls gave way to painted plaster. They passed through the section that housed the King's Guard, where Dominic Richelieu himself had once had an office.

Greg found himself wishing that he could tell his friends the truth about himself and where he'd really come from, but he knew he couldn't. How could he possibly explain that he wasn't from the distant town of Artagnan at all— but was instead from four hundred years in the future? Or that Michel Dinicoeur and Dominic Richelieu were actually the same person? Or that Michel was an immortal madman who'd traveled back through time to kill the Musketeers as revenge for something they hadn't even done yet?

As they climbed a wide wooden staircase, the Louvre suddenly became alive with activity. Greg had always assumed that the palace was only the king's home, but in fact hundreds of servants lived there as well—including the Musketeers themselves. The route took Greg right past their quarters. It was a small room and they all had to share it, but compared to the living conditions of most people in 1615 Paris, the accommodations were amazing. The boys all had beds to sleep on, rather than mere thatches of straw. And there was even indoor plumbing—as long as they didn't mind going down the hall and using a communal— and coed—bathroom that didn't have a lock on the door.

Greg's parents' room was right next door to his. King Louis had graciously allowed them to move into the castle as well after their rescue from La Mort. The door currently hung open, revealing that Greg's parents weren't in. Greg was wondering where they'd gone when Aramis burst out of the Musketeers' quarters.

"D'Artagnan!" he crowed. "Just who I wanted to see! You'll never believe what I learned today!"

"Actually, can it wait?" Greg asked. "The king asked to see me."

"I'll walk with you. It's too exciting." Aramis dropped in beside Greg and held up a tiny scrap of black fabric. It was two inches long, an inch wide, and torn on three sides— as though it had been ripped from a piece of clothing. "Remember this?"

"Of course," Greg said. "I found it."

The shred of fabric was the only clue the boys had to Dominic and Michel's whereabouts. A few months earlier, Michel had forced Milady de Winter to deliver a letter to a messenger at an inn. Under questioning later, Milady claimed that she had no idea what was in the letter or where the messenger was from—only that he was a foreigner. Aramis had believed her—but then, Aramis was smitten with Milady. Athos hadn't believed her at all—but then, Athos was also smitten with Milady, and he knew she liked Aramis more than she liked him.

The day after Dominic had escaped from prison, Greg had asked Milady to take him to the inn. She had led all the Musketeers there on horseback. The inn only had a single room for guests, and there Greg had found the scrap of cloth snagged on a jagged splinter of wood that jutted from the wall. The innkeeper's wife said it *looked* like it was from the clothes the mysterious man had worn.

"It's silk," Aramis said proudly, as he and Greg followed King Louis's messenger through the palace.

"So?" Greg asked.

Aramis frowned. "Is silk not a big deal in the future?"

Greg thought about the clothes his family had owned. His mother had several silk dresses and his father probably had some silk ties as well. "I don't think it's cheap, but I don't think it's rare, either."

"Well, it's rare here. And expensive. Silk comes all the way from the Far East, and only a few shipments reach Europe every year. What arrives tends to stay in the port cities—usually Venice or Barcelona. Only the tiniest amounts of silk ever make it to Paris."

Greg stopped walking and examined the scrap of silk more closely. "So whoever Milady met at the inn that night was no common messenger?"

"Exactly. Anyone wearing such fancy clothes would most likely be the emissary representing the king of a foreign nation."

Greg's heart thumped in his chest. France was surrounded by countries that were always on the verge of invading: England, Spain, the duchies of Italy, and the Habsburg Empire, which controlled Germany, Switzerland, and the Netherlands. If Dominic had dealings with *any* of them, it was reason for concern. "Which one?"

"I don't know yet." Aramis took the scrap of silk back and carefully tucked it away. "I need to figure out where this silk was made. I'll bet a month's wages that, wherever it is, Dominic and Michel have fled there."

"But we don't know that for sure," Greg said.

"No," Aramis admitted. "Still, this is the best lead we have."

"How long will it take to find out where the silk is from?"

"A few days—if we're lucky."

Greg silently cursed the backward age in which he was trapped. What would have taken five seconds to discover with a simple Wikipedia search could take *forever* to find out in the past. "There's no way to do it any faster?" he asked. "With every day that goes by, Michel and Dominic are getting closer and closer to . . ."

He caught himself at the last second, not wanting to mention the Devil's Stone before the king's messenger. Aramis recognized the worry in Greg's eyes, though. "Allow us a moment?" he asked the messenger, then pulled Greg into a small alcove where they could speak in peace.

"I know that finding the stone is of utmost importance to you," Aramis whispered. "I'm doing everything I can to figure out where it is. Over the past two months, I've combed through every book, scroll, and parchment in Paris. . . ."

"And you haven't found a single mention of it?" Greg

asked. "There must be something somewhere. I mean, Michel had to learn about the stone somewhere, back when he was Dominic. . . ."

"Well," Aramis said hesitantly, "I did find *something* a few days ago . . ."

"And you didn't tell me?" Greg couldn't contain himself in his excitement.

"It was merely an oblique reference," Aramis whispered, signaling Greg to keep his voice down. "It didn't even mention the Devil's Stone by name."

"What was it?"

"I found it in a scroll in the archives at Notre Dame. It was a transcript of the travels of a monk who stayed there two hundred years ago." Until Greg had met him, Aramis himself had been a cleric at Notre Dame, responsible for transcribing texts from one language to another. The cathedral had the largest library in the city. "He mentioned hearing about a magic stone with incredible powers that was last seen in the White City of Emperor Constantine."

"What's the White City of Emperor Constantine?" Greg asked.

"I don't know," Aramis admitted. "And neither does anyone else I've talked to. There were several Emperor Constantines in the Roman era, but they all lived more than a thousand years ago. . . ."

Greg felt all the excitement drain from him.

Aramis put a comforting hand on his arm. "Don't

despair," he said. "We'll find the stone. I promise you that."

Despite his reassuring tone, Greg still felt hollow inside. "We *have* to," he said. "No offense, but I can't stay in this time forever."

"I know," Aramis told him. "I'm doing everything I can. . . ."

Before he could go on, the messenger coughed impatiently out in the hall. "Monsieur D'Artagnan. The *king* still waits for you."

Greg nodded, then told Aramis, "The sooner you can find out about that silk, the better. I'll take any lead I can get." He then followed the messenger down another hall to a set of large, imposing wooden doors flanked by two members of the King's Guard.

The messenger bowed subserviently before them. "At the king's request, I have brought Monsieur D'Artagnan."

The guards dramatically opened the doors and Greg passed into the throne room.

He had been inside it often—in fact, this was the very room he had landed in after jumping through time—and yet he never could get past how dull it was. It was so vast that the oil lamps barely made a dent in the darkness, though they did create a grimy slick of burnt oil on the walls and ceiling.

Louis XIII was slumped in his throne. The king was only fourteen, like Greg. He'd taken the throne at the age of nine when his father was assassinated, and he still gave the impression of a young boy merely pretending to be king. His formal royal red gown, trimmed with ermine, swallowed him up.

"D'Artagnan!" Louis said. "Thank goodness you've come. . . ."

"I'm sorry it took so long, Your Majesty," Greg began. "I was practicing my sword-fighting skills all the way at the other end of—"

"I don't care about your tardiness. I care about my safety. I've just learned some terrifying news." Louis sat upright, his eyes boring into Greg's. "Someone in my family is plotting to kill me."